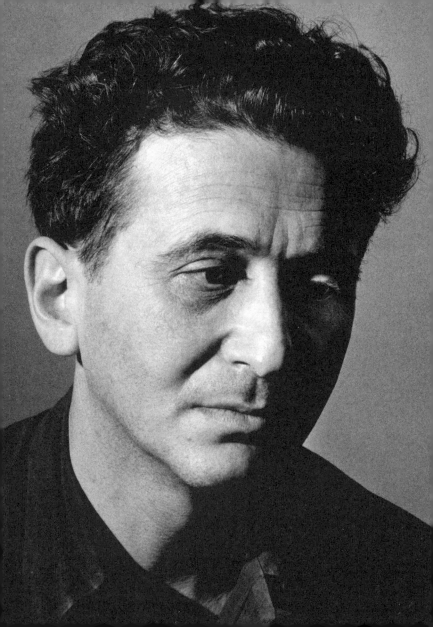

EGON HOSTOVSKÝ

THE
HIDEOUT

Translated from the Czech
by Fern Long

PUSHKIN PRESS

LONDON

Pushkin Press
71–75 Shelton Street
London, WC2H 9JQ

The Hideout was first published in the US in 1945

The Hideout was first published as *Úkryt* in Czechoslovakia in 1946

First published by Pushkin Press in 2017

1 3 5 7 9 8 6 4 2

ISBN 978 1 78227 240 3

Frontispiece: by courtesy of Olga Hostovská

Text designed and typeset by Tetragon, London

Proudly printed and bound in Great Britain by
TJ International, Padstow, Cornwall

www.pushkinpress.com

THE
HIDEOUT

I

Dearest Hanichka:

A T LAST I can hope that some day you will learn the true facts of my strange story. The good people about whom I want to tell you promise me that they can take my notes somewhere to safety, somewhere beyond the ocean, perhaps, and give them to you after the war is over. You are still alive; I don't doubt that for an instant, and you will be alive long after this awful storm of horror, madness and hunger has blown over. I am absolutely certain of it. I see you all the time; we're together whenever I fall asleep; I know every new line that creases your face; I know that your hair is white and that you are bent now. Dear God, I know so many details about you—just as if we were together and saw each other day in and day out. You have been waiting, and not in vain, dear Hanichka! Some day you will read what I am writing now. Otherwise nothing would have any meaning, nothing at all—our life, our marriage, our worries and our mistakes. But I don't believe that, and it is not so. Everything has its meaning, every event, every chance, every catastrophe, every slightest thing that happens.

You must live to get this, because you and I have to understand each other. And it is only now that I am ready to understand you. I have come to know so much, so much has become clear, I have found so many words and thoughts that I never even knew of before.

I don't know if they will tell it to you after the war, or if they will write it to you. It may even be that you will learn of it only from these notes—from this paragraph. I, Hanichka, shall not live to know. It seems so silly to write that I want to die, or that I must die. I don't really know how to tell you in just a few words that we can never meet again and live together and make up for all the things we did to hurt each other, and be happy together in the lives of our children. It would be ridiculous if I tried to make my death appear heroic. It isn't altogether voluntary and perhaps it isn't inevitable, but it is natural.

Please keep on reading; don't let yourself go. It truly means nothing at all that I shall no longer be living at the moment you read these lines. It's so long since you've seen me; you've probably buried me and wept for me many times over in your imagination. Truly it is nothing, my darling! I am closer to you, and I shall be closer, than I was when I lived beside you.

There, now I have written it. You know it and I feel much better. Look, until a short while ago, I had one fixed image. I saw my return and our meeting. I dreamed that we met again in Rokytnice, in the home of your parents. The door

8

there still opens with difficulty and creaks; along the walls of the entry, casks and boxes are still piled, and it's always cold twilight there. Of course you aren't expecting me. I come back quite unannounced; you call from the kitchen: "Is that you, Father?" I don't answer, because I can't. You ask again and then you come out across the threshold; you come farther, you walk down several steps—and then you see me and recognize me. I see it all so plainly! You want to lift your arms, but you can't; you want to cry out, but you only whisper. It is not my name that you whisper. For a while I am frozen to the spot. We are both deathly pale, and we feel as if we were dying. The air between us is not of this earth. You start to collapse, and that gives me strength. I am beside you in a bound and catch you in my arms. You don't cry and you don't smile. You only whisper that word, which is not my name.

A hundred times, a thousand times, I have imagined, dreamed and lived our meeting. I could picture everything: the twilight of the passage, the smell of it, the sound of your steps on the stairs, myself and you. There is only one thing that I can not imagine: the pain that would close around our hearts and throats while our hands sought each other and met. Everything but that dizzy feeling of happiness, or unhappiness, or some deep feeling without a name.

Would it be happiness, or would it be unhappiness? I don't really know. I don't know what my first words would be; I don't know what I would ask about, whom I would look for; I don't know where I would sit, what I would do with my hands and my memory and my will. And still I never longed for anything more than I have longed for our meeting and for that unimaginable something that would come after it. When I thought of my return, about that unredeemed miracle, I felt that I would be capable of doing anything to make it come true—capable of every sacrifice and every crime. Not from longing and not from exhaustion, but from a kind of burning curiosity, more burning than any longing or desire I ever knew.

But today I know, Hanichka, that I was dreaming of the impossible—as I have done so many times before. I should bring you no happiness from far away. I should come back to you, old before my time (I'll soon be fifty) a man whose story would seem like senseless gibberish to you. I should be a hindrance to you and our children. (Ah, I know nothing at all about them! Marta is twenty and Johanna eighteen, I believe? I think of them shamefully little, and I don't see them even in my dreams. I lost them and they lost me.) Well, I should be returning to a life where something had been lacking while I lived it. I should be returning to it out of a bad fairy tale, without the golden key and the elixir of life. There would be an emptiness between us and I shouldn't know how to fill it. All the love I am able to wring out of my desolate heart, all the feeling and devotion I may be putting into these lines, is released in me only because I know that I shall soon die. It is the knowledge that I have found the right ending for my ordinary life, and that happiness lies in renunciation, and peace where there is no fear of death. I wish I could say it in some other way; I wish that I could let you look into my thoughts which are so much clearer, so much less brittle than the sentences I have just written! But I believe that with all my clumsiness I shall still find words now and then that I should not have found before, and words that will find their way to your understanding.

The most important thing of all is that you should know at the very beginning that I did not run away from you. I did not say good-bye to you and the children because I thought I should be coming back in a few days, but I was kept from doing that by events. Later on, as I write, I want to explain all that to you too, if I have time to do it. I don't know if I'll be able to finish this little notebook, and so I'm going to put down the most important things first and then come back to the details later.

On March 10, 1939, I did not go to Ostrava, as I told you at the time, but I flew to Paris. Immediately after Prague was occupied I found out that the Germans had a warrant for my arrest. I was afraid for you and the children and that is why I neither wrote to you nor sent you any message. In France I lived off the beaten track, and most likely none of the other Czechs knew—or knows—where I finally disappeared. When France was collapsing, the Paris police arrested me by mistake. They set me free after they had kept me for a week, and by then the Germans were at my heels. I didn't get any farther away from Paris than a little village in Normandy, where I sought out my old friend, Dr. Aubin. I think I must have told you about him long ago. This fine Frenchman took pity on me and proposed a fantastic scheme: to hide me in his home for the duration of the war. I agreed to this. And from that day to this I have been living in a little cellar with one window, through which you can see nothing, and a chink in the wall, through which you can see very little. I eat, after a fashion, I read the papers, sometimes I listen to the radio, but I hardly ever hear a human voice, and I seldom see a human being flit by outside. Dr. Aubin comes to me only at night, in the dark. I have been living in this prison since the second half of June, 1940. Now it is May, 1942.

At the end of last April something happened. You could hardly imagine, let alone believe, what I did. How should I tell you? I'll come back to this later, but in the meantime— well, I killed a man. He was a man I knew, and it wasn't in self-defense. Yes, God forgive me, that's the truth! I had to kill him, even though I had never harmed even a chicken up to that moment. It happened when I came out of my hideout for the first time. I pulled the body into my cellar and lived with it a night and a day and a night, and still a day, for it was that long before Dr. Aubin came back to me. When he finally did come, he found me in a terrible state and he himself was horrified at the death. It was on my account, or rather, on account of the dead man in his cellar, that he had to tell his secret to the underground. They got rid of the corpse but discovered me. When they found out that I was an engineer they asked me to undertake a suicidal thing. At first I would not agree to it. But then all at once many things became clear to me and I realized that God himself had sent these people to me. At first I could not understand why everyone wanted me to die: the Germans and the French people in the underground, friends and enemies. But suddenly I understood, and I promised to do it. I haven't the slightest hope that I'll come out alive but, even so, please don't think I'm any hero. I shall do what I have to do gladly, even though I may not fully agree with it. After all, someone must sacrifice himself, you know, and I am doing it first of all for myself, and then for you. If I didn't do it, probably nothing in the world would change, only I shouldn't be able to tell you everything as I am doing now, and I should die somewhere alone and forsaken, and the past would weigh me down terribly. Now I feel so light—almost as if I could fly. Everything between you and me is so very clear; all at once Dr. Aubin is more than a friend, and these strange Frenchmen are like my brothers and I can imagine real peace, yours and my own and our children's. And this unearthly, exultant glory of victory that I carry around in myself no one can ever know!

Only God knows how I was able to live in this hole for so long. Alone, alone, always alone! My fear of death must have been stronger than my fear of emptiness, of constant hunger and cold. Besides, my prison was a natural sequel to all my life that had gone before. Even before I had been in constant solitude; even before it had been as if my best friends came to me in the dark, and as if I very seldom saw a human face.

Don't get the idea, Hanichka, that I know nothing of what's going on in the world. I hear the Paris radio from the neighboring houses at least once a month, if it's on loud enough and if the people leave their windows open. Dr. Aubin often brought his radio down here and we listened to London. Several times we even heard the Czech broadcast. My host brings me the newspapers, so that I keep informed on all the really important happenings. But no matter what I hear, no matter what I read, I have to translate it all into a new language which only I understand. You know, it's something like this: if someone says the word space, other people think of something quite different to what a person of my training thinks of. I know that space is the unimaginable essence of the universe, bound up inseparably with whatever goes on—because I am a mathematician and a physicist, and a mathematician and physicist with very special training, at that. How could I ever come to an understanding about space with a man who imagines something quite concrete when he hears the word space? And, you see, that's how it is with the echo of the world which reaches me here. It tells me only that there is a terrible war on earth raging between several worlds. And that in this war it is a question now of something quite different to what it was in the beginning, and at the end it will be a question of something quite different to what it is today. This war, I think, broke out and is being fought from causes and for aims which no one has yet been able to express clearly. I keep having the feeling that a good half of the human race got drunk in a kind of gigantic space where the air is all breathed out. The born fighters and brawlers started to fight in their drunken orgy, and they were helped along and encouraged by the drunken hypocrites. And all at once the fight spread like wild fire until it touched everyone. By now, thank God, we have advanced far enough so that we can tell our friends from our enemies, but the drunkenness lasts, the guilt is still debatable and the harm done is beyond imagination.

I got mixed up in the mêlée without rhyme or reason. I was living the quiet life of a peace-loving citizen; I never betrayed anyone; I didn't drink; I didn't smoke; I paid my taxes and I was a respecter of the law; I didn't meddle in politics. My brain isn't big enough to grasp and realize all the catastrophes which kept me from returning home, going on with my work, taking care of my wife and children. I was certainly not responsible for any of it, and I never deserved to have to live worse than a dog, not allowed to leave my kennel, not allowed to work, not allowed to speak in an ordinary voice, and not allowed ever to eat my fill or to get warm enough. And still I do not have the right merely to wait and sleep through the storm in my hideout.

Now I have come to the most troublesome point in my story. And it's the point that means the most to me. As long as I was running away and hiding from death my head was empty. What could I do, what could I do? Some voice kept crying out in me: why all this? You're innocent! And the echo of the world told me nothing. Then I did not know the language into which I could translate it for my heart. What could I do? If I left my shelter, the Germans would catch me and torture me to death. Try to get to England? How? Dr. Aubin couldn't help me. Turn to the French underground, which my host scarcely knew? They couldn't use me; they couldn't use anyone who had to hide.

And while I was torturing myself, thinking, not sleeping, losing my mind, my fate was mounting to its climax. I had forgotten, that is, that even my crippled life and my fantastic role were only parts of the great drama going on outside myself. And you can't run away from that drama, Hanichka. A person can't escape himself, people, God and the world all at once. No matter how he hides himself, he's still in the play. Every move he makes is measured and weighed somewhere. But some understanding can exist between subject and object. If I had only known and understood in time, I should have been able to wait for my right moment patiently and I shouldn't have tormented myself with vain questioning. The right moment comes to every life—only to recognize it! Only not to miss that instant when it depends on us whether we shall unite ourselves forever with mankind and the universe, or whether we shall change into the wandering shadows of shadows! Only not to sleep through that time when we can step out from the wings and recite our soliloquy irrevocably, and play our part well!

I don't know how these French conspirators understand my decision, how Dr. Aubin understands it, and how that man, whose voice I often hear on the London broadcast, would understand it. But that doesn't matter. It's more important that what I am doing gives me that infectious strength which is needed to tame the raging elements. My decision opens a new way to an almost mystic communion with the people whom I came to know only a short time ago, and it definitely returns me somehow to those long-ago days, almost beyond remembrance, when life still had all the marks of sublimity and glory, when dreams had halos and when faith dubbed us knights.

With a sort of premonition, long before my fate was decided, I turned back to my childhood again and again, to the very threshold of that lost Paradise, for it is only from there that you can start afresh. Change into a child, and you change the world! Perhaps those who make the echo of the world and whose speech I have to translate for myself, would find that I have gone mad; others would say that I am a suicide, and others still that I am a hero. Or a criminal, a murderer, a coward. What do I know? What does it matter? What does anything at all matter, if I can forget everything with which I grew old, and if I can march forward with a manly stride to meet my greatest adventure, at whose end you will be smiling, and our children, and my new friends, and all the unknown living and dead who bear the escutcheon of poverty and the shield of misery, those eternal soldiers for whom, from the beginning of the world until today, no archangel ever trumpeted a summons to a truce?

2

I N THE EMPTINESS of my hideout I have often tortured myself with the question: wouldn't everything between us have turned out differently if only I could have made up my mind to talk with you? You were a good wife to me, Hanichka, and probably I was a good husband to you. But were we happy? At the moment when that question first occurred to me I should have spoken, I should have looked for words and ways to keep from happening the thing which did happen—that in the end I should vanish into emptiness, disappear like a thief, drop out of sight just as suddenly as I appeared before you twenty-one years ago. If only I had spoken! If only at the eleventh hour unthinking crowds of people could speak one with the other—people whose lives may have all the signs of being full—all, except happiness. Just imagine the unplumbed sources of strength which might be released in time to protect and save the people!

Do you know when I felt absolutely certain that something was wrong in my work, in my marriage, in my plans, in everything that I was saying or doing? That first night of our last vacation in July, 1938. Do you remember that little red villa on the shores of the Luzhnice? I can see it before me now, as plainly as if I had just walked through its front door. And I can see all the people who stayed there in such thorough detail that it makes my head swim. Just as when you meet your dead relatives in your dreams. Both of us got tired early that evening, after our trip, but I didn't feel like going to sleep. About eight o'clock you went upstairs to our room—I think you were reading—and both of our daughters sat out on the terrace with two students. I remember that Marta's laughter upset me that night; it was a new kind of laughter, forced and no longer childish. I stood under a low-branched apple tree a few feet away from the villa, on the path that leads to the woods. The old attorney Malina (was that his name?) was with me and he was telling me some family story in confidence. He was smoking a cigar, he stammered and talked like a foreigner, because he had an extraordinarily small vocabulary. He was always saying something wrong or out of place, "with apologies," and his favorite word was "quasi." This old man, whom I came to know only that afternoon, after our arrival, suddenly turned all my thoughts upside down.

"You know, sir, today I can say it: I am completely happy. Absolutely nothing is lacking in my life. My children are quasi taken care of, my health is still like iron—but why keep on talking? A completely happy man stands before you!"

Would you believe, Hanichka, that until that moment no one had ever told me that he was completely happy? It froze me. I felt envy, and a kind of indefinable discontent at the same time. I excused myself and left the loquacious attorney. I ran into the children in the doorway. Marta hid her hands behind her back quickly, but not before I saw that she was holding a cigarette in her fingers.

"Are you going to bed already, Papa?"

"Yes, and…"

No, I said nothing to her. Suddenly she was a stranger to me—that unnatural laughter, the cigarette, that "Papa"! But that was what the children called me all the time! Only a short while ago I should have been very angry if I had caught Marta smoking. Now I scarcely gave it a second thought. I muttered something about the lateness of the hour and went on, until the surprised and annoyed voices of both girls stopped me:

"But it isn't nine o'clock yet, Papa!"

I turned around—and I think that then I saw them for the last time as they really were. A little turned away from the homeward path. With a flash of discontent in their eyes. In comic dancing poses. They would still have come running to me if I had stretched out my arms to them, they could still have forgotten that they had just wanted to walk out into the firefly-lighted darkness. In their gaze were childhood, whisperings, lullabies, fairy tales. In their dancing poses there was already time which had taken them from me. Yes, then I saw them for the last time as they really were. Our children, our waking nights, Hanichka, our torment, our likeness, our lives with a different fate. For a few seconds they looked at the graying man on whose lap it was no longer proper to climb, from whom their secrets must be hidden, and who was always kind and good (mostly at Christmas and on birthdays), but also strict and cold (for example, at the end of the school year), who had a very strange occupation and ludicrous and annoying habits, who worried so unnecessarily when they were ill, couldn't endure their tears, liked their dresses and their books, gave them money much more readily than their mother, and was so adorably old-fashioned, just as if he had been cut out of a child's reader.

In that instant I sensed that I was parting with them, that our paths were dividing. My anxiety, which until then had been smoldering, suddenly burst into flame. What is it? I thought, and with all my strength tore my legs, which seemed turned to wood, from the steps. And really, later on I could see our children only through my own cares, and through the ruins of my real and apparent certainties, which had begun to fall down around us.

You were already sleeping, but the light was still burning on the night table and a book bound in green lay on a chair with your clothes. I undressed quietly. Then I sat down on the bed and mechanically reached for the book. It was the stories of a young Czech writer. Simple, pious little stories about the country. I leafed through the book and felt my disquiet grow. It was as if the author were warning the reader on every page of the terrible cloud that was gathering over the earth. As if, looking from human fate to the quietness of the skies at night, he heard the human ants lament, and saw their dwellings in ruins. The strange book of a strange, believing author! It was called *Whitsuntide*.

It occurred to me that most of the books of the younger authors I had read recently fatigue the mind with their dark, obscure heroes and their sense of fate. As if life were to end at any minute, and as if adventurers, dreamers, saints and sinners were all in a blind alley together. Where does our literary youth get its strange fear and its auguries of ill omen? In that green-bound book I read a sentence which I remember to this day:

"Everything is as uncertain as it was then, and footsteps in the people's path through the dust of this country are still more confused. The instruments of destruction are more infernal."

I read these lines several times, and then the last words of the story: *"But our breath is cut down from day to day and the space of our body and soul is narrowed to the coffin."*

I slammed the book shut, and glanced at you as you slept, quietly breathing and smiling a little at some pleasant dream. Your nightgown had slipped from your shoulders. Automatically I reached for the blanket, to pull it up over you, but then I thought better of it and watched your breast rise and fall, and how the wrinkles on your forehead had smoothed away, and how you grew younger under my eyes. I lay down beside you carefully and brought my lips close to the light current of your breath. I awakened you, but only half. You opened your eyes, the wrinkles sprang out on your forehead again, you quickly pulled the blanket up over your half-naked breast, and closed your eyes again. I put out the light.

"I am completely happy!" some voice kept repeating mockingly in me after the old attorney. Oh, it was a bad night! Blind, full of nightmare forebodings, heavy and fainting. Drops of sweat broke out on my forehead because I remembered something I never liked to recall. Your tears, when we were first married, the green letter which you once hid from me, so many, many unsaid things between us. Is she happy? And are you happy? Ill-spoken attorney! And Marta smokes and laughs almost—shamelessly! And—and my wife has certainly been unfaithful to me! This sentence, said half-aloud, ambushed the remnants of my equilibrium. I groaned. Clenching my fists convulsively, I went on listening to the ugly soliloquy. You live like a marionette. Figures and wheels and joyless puritanism make your world. Somehow, to no purpose, you have your wife and your children and your friends around you. And you are hopelessly in love with another woman; you know who, don't deny it! You are pitiable and ridiculous! Whenever you meet Madame Olga your ears turn red; that's all you can do. You enjoy reading sentimental stories of great love, kept secret until death. Why, for example, do you always keep Hamsun's *Victoria* within arm's reach in your library? Because you love no one but Hanna? Then try something! Take her in your arms now,

awaken her and tell her everything you are feeling. Say:
My Hanichka (you couldn't do it?), something is happening
within me and outside myself. Please, let's stand together
now; there's something hanging in mid-air, something's
preparing to fall on us; it's bad, I feel it, I know it, Hanna,
Hanichka. No matter what has happened in the past, we're
nearest to each other, together we must…

I did something altogether out of the ordinary. I got up,
dressed in the dark and slipped out of the room like a thief.
As I walked along the terrace, shrouded in darkness, I heard
Marta's muffled voice:

"Do you think he loves me?"

Johanna answered slowly and hesitantly:

"He must love you, if he kissed you."

I stood there petrified. He must love you, if he kissed you!
The muscles around my mouth hurt from an uncontrollable,
numb smile. My poor, stupid little girl! He must love you,
if he kissed you… I started toward them quickly, holding
back my tears, but I didn't go very far. They'd be frightened
if I should suddenly start to embrace and kiss them like a
madman. And in the end I'd blubber; no, they mustn't see
me like this! What was happening to me?

It was a starry night; trees and buildings looked like
hobgoblins. A breeze laden with damp smells blew from
the river and every one of those smells awakened some
soundly sleeping memory. I walked aimlessly, dulled by the
air and the flickering of the darkness. I had already walked

through this maze in fear, I had already lived this night, but when and where?

The long-drawn-out voice of a harmonica led me on. I followed after it in a kind of trance. The smells of the water and leaves grew, and with them the memories from far away multiplied too. I stumbled through this night of bewitching summer and of my own life. The deceptive rustling of the dark and its smell played a magic game with time. Every erring step after the uncapturable past was a step in a seven-league boot. With lightning speed I crossed the pallid distances of the past.

"I can't sleep," I said out loud, and pulled up short at the sound of my own voice. By then I was already sitting in the tavern over a glass of suspiciously red lemonade, next to the famous guest of our villa, the composer Nosek. You certainly have not forgotten him, Hanichka! The place was smoky, and overflowing with a grotesque mixture of half-drunken villagers and vacationers from the cities. Someone was playing a harmonica at the bar, and on a little polished square under a garish chandelier three perspiring couples were dancing.

"I can't sleep either," said the composer Nosek—and all at once I was glad that I could be sitting beside that famous man and speaking with him. "The devil knows what it is. Maybe it is war being presaged by sleeplessness."

"I don't believe that war will break out, sir." I said that only out of an unpleasant habit of protesting.

"And I believe it will! Oh, if only that lad with the harmonica would give us peace! I don't believe in comets, you know—but I believe in people, in their way of walking, their haste, their dances, their gestures… Sir, the rhythm of this dirty, overcrowded place is different to how it was years ago, and different to how it was only a short time ago. I've been coming here for the summer for twelve years now. I can tell what's in the air by watching the people around me. The rhythms of their lives, do you understand? In this respect I am a diviner. But wait a minute, we have a local clairvoyant here; he tells your fortune with cards, but he may be half gone by now. Mr. Vydra, come over here and reveal our future!"

A bearded, ragged fellow, hardly able to stand on his feet, fumbled around with a deck of dirty cards and then told us that there would be a terrible war, long and bloody, but that we would both live through it, and that both of us would be rich and famous, and wouldn't the gentlemen pay by buying him a whiskey?

"Now we really should go home to sleep," said Nosek, and stood up. The city people at the surrounding tables recognized him for the first time, craned their necks, and some of them greeted him with noisy ostentation. For an instant I felt warmed by the consciousness that I was with a famous man. He had blinking, ironical eyes which winked meaningfully at me when I handed him his hat and stick. I blushed at my vanity, for it occurred to me that Nosek saw through it. But nevertheless—oh, how petty I used to be!—I felt a new wave of joy when the composer linked arms with me.

"Do you know why we can't sleep?" he asked in a small, changed voice when we came out of the inn. He had a habit of stopping every few steps, to emphasize his words. We were standing in pitch darkness just then, and we couldn't see each other's faces. But I would have wagered my head on it—he wasn't smiling then.

"We're afraid, friend, that's why we don't sleep! And it isn't the war we're afraid of—it's something else. What do you think it is? I'd certainly like to work out what it is we're so terribly afraid of!"

Quietly and in the dark I went back to you, threw my clothes off and lay down. This time I fell asleep very soon, but woke up often. Toward morning I had a remarkably vivid dream.

I was walking with you, Hanichka, and the children, along the tracks that passed through the lost country of my childhood. I recognized every tree, every stone, and later I remembered that it was that countryside which the smell of the night had tried in vain to resurrect when I ran away from you, overheard our daughters' conversation, and then wandered along the path after the Pied Piper with the harmonica. At the right of the tracks I saw in my dream a pond where rushes grew, and at the left a spruce forest. And then I saw the house of the station-master, Mr. Andrejs, who always stood at attention by his door when a train passed by, and saluted. I saw his garden, the fence, the yard as big as your palm, with its rabbit hutch and three chickens. It was after sunset, and we were walking along the track with knapsacks on our backs. The warm breeze was full of an unearthly balminess, twilight fell soothingly over the earth in blue veils, every step was a joy to the heart, every draft of air fired the blood, everything the eye saw was good and merciful.

But suddenly a thunderous noise echoed in the distance, as if a giant train were coming toward us on the track, full of infernal monsters. The noise was made by things animate and inanimate: there was the splintering of breaking glass in it, the crackling of flames, the howling of dogs, the croaking of frogs, the lament of boughs broken in a storm, the roar of water that has broken a dam, the crying of babies, the shrieks of hysterical women and the groaning of the wounded. The roar came nearer. Our hearts stopped beating from fear. I gathered you and the children in my arms, we clung together convulsively, we merged in one flesh, one feeling, one thought.

Mr. Andrejs came running out of his house. He had a lantern in his hand, he ran along the track and cried out in a shrill voice, cracking with terror, one very strange word: "Karutmon! The Karutmon is coming! Run! The Karutmon!"

The strangest thing is that I understood that word in my dream—and now I no longer understand it. I knew what the Karutmon was. Without a doubt it was something loathsome, something within people and outside them too.

"Throw everything away!" I shouted to you and the children. "Let's pray, let's not leave one another, come closer to me, we must have only one head and one mouth, otherwise we shall suffocate!"

We stood there before that onslaught of horror, and grew into one another in quiet sorrow and we lived with one blood and with one heart and we loved one another desperately. We all understood what the word Karutmon meant. It came rolling toward us—darkness, waters, fire, excrement, mangled bodies, blood and a sea of moans and roars. And we stood in it like a rock, grown together; we still lived, still realized and understood that only our shared breath and our shared heart would save us. It was hideous and beautiful too. We were born again. We were four-in-one. We grew above the mounting flood of that terrible element that was called Karutmon.

And then I woke up. I could still taste horror on my tongue, and the world was still falling away before my eyes. But in my quick breathing and in the racing of my heart there was such love as had never been there before.

"Hanna!" I cried.

You came running from the bathroom in flight. You were naked, only pressing a towel to your breast.

I stretched out my arms to you, but the horror was melting on my tongue, and I stopped seeing the world falling to pieces. I came to completely, and sobered up.

"Forgive me," I said, forcing a laugh. "I had a bad dream, and I must have cried out in my sleep."

Deftly you threw some kind of robe around you, and you laughed too.

"You frightened me so! What was your dream anyway?"

You said the last words thoughtfully, and as if you were disappointed. I rubbed my temples. I was completely myself and I thought about what I always thought whenever I wanted to escape my worries and improve a bad mood: about my sight for anti-aircraft guns. And I repeated proudly to myself—as I did every morning—a stereotyped sentence: That little gadget could decide the next war!

Then I remembered my confusion of yesterday again, and growled angrily to myself: Nerves!

You were back in the bathroom and the door was ajar.

"Hanna!" I called, and came in after you. "Our Marta is smoking. I caught her at it yesterday. That must stop at once!"

3

M Y MEMORY is not miraculous, Hanichka, but some of the details of the past have been so firmly fixed in my thoughts. To this day I cannot measure and weigh the whole drama, and, if I still sometimes try to, I go to pieces. My brain is quite paralyzed when it has to cope with larger segments of time. All the collective unhappiness and all the collective catastrophes from the time of the mobilization, of Munich, and the ruining of our country, I can see only in little flashes, as if they were lit up by lightning in a great dark space, in an atmosphere of fever and in a chaos without sequence. Something like this: A stammering creature shouts, "P-p-put out your lights!" An unwatched child cries in front of a house with darkened windows. A confused bookkeeper adds his expenses and his receipts all in one column. The loudspeaker bellows into dead silence, "Keep quiet!" An officer throws his sword into the river. A riderless horse gallops through the streets of Prague. An endless mob of beggars plays blindman's buff on Václavské Náměstí and sings a song that has only one word: "Arms!" But amongst these confused pictures in black and white, I still see narrow glimpses of bygone scenes. There are only a few such scenes which have a kind of breadth and depth, a few views of that life which have been caught on the border of the shadows by a kind of miracle. Prague in those days seems a windowless refuge; nevertheless there are chinks through which I can see fragments of the story, and for me it is a breathtaking view of a chessboard where unknown forces, out of caprice and cruel curiosity, set up live chessmen, endowed with free will, and allowed them to play out one of the variations of the ancient tragi-comedy. At one of these views I have already stopped innumerable times in my excursions into the not-distant past. Return to it with me, Hanichka. It is a day at the end of February, in 1939.

We were expecting guests for supper: my chief, my secretary from the factory, and Madame Olga. What a bizarre trio! A chill goes up my spine when I try now to follow the hidden threads of chance which seated us two and our three guests at the table for a simple supper and a conversation in cryptogram. In that inconspicuous gathering each one of the participants followed his own secret plan, and played his own secret role within himself. Five people met—to establish that their common will was enough. But each of them was being dragged by an invisible rope to another drama and tried to take his neighbor along at least part of the way. In the course of time and by dint of sharp observation, I was able to see through all the roles of that evening—all except yours, Hanichka. Perhaps you alone were not playing a game of chess. But who knows?

I remember that you were rather nervous when I came home from the factory. You had sent both the girls to the theater. You sat in the library at the window, you were knitting a sweater and watching me out of the corner of your eye. I was very upset and pretended to read.

"What kind of a man is that director of yours?" you asked, looking thoughtfully at the ceiling, as if you were thinking about something else. That wasn't the question I was afraid of, and so I answered with extreme alacrity.

"I don't know much about him. A hard worker, a stickler and a splendid organizer. He's a little loud, but I think that's because he's shy. He really invited himself; he said that we ought to talk privately some time and, besides, that he'd like to meet my wife. I don't know what he's after. Maybe nothing at all."

"I doubt it! What's his name?"

"Schwartz, Engineer Schwartz. Don't call him by any title; he doesn't like it. Plain Mr. Schwartz will do. And please [I could feel my ears turning red again] let's not talk about politics, or Jews, or about what's going to happen, on account of Madame Olga. Do you understand?"

You put your knitting away and took a book off the shelf very casually. Then you drew a deep breath and said in that quiet voice, which I never knew, and never tried to find out, whether it was really as indifferent as it sounded:

"Isn't it really only panic that makes her want to go away and try to find work in France?"

"No, it is not! It's going to be very bad for the Jews here, no matter what happens. And she's still young, don't you think so? A widow, with no children... But let's not talk about all this, or we'll find ourselves discussing it at supper whether we want to or not. And what good would it do? She's coming to say good-bye to us, so why upset her for the last time?"

"I'm very fond of her."

I said nothing.

"And I like Anna too, the poor thing. The other day she stopped here with the briefcase you forgot at the office. All of a sudden I felt so sorry for her! Without her two canes she is quite lame—she can't take a step. But her face is lovely; she certainly would have married if it weren't for those legs. Now I'll go set the table. Come along with me and talk to me!"

Whenever you asked me to talk to you I always became completely mute. At that time too, every sound from the outside took the words from your lips, every noise, every ringing or knocking. What's happening again? Some kind of demonstration? What did they announce over the radio? That the Germans are cutting off our electricity? Who announced it? That our theaters are going to be closed and meetings forbidden? Martial law? Impossible! Both thoughts and people were going around in circles; everything seemed useless, stupid, futile—but you know very well how it was.

I walked after you from the kitchen to the dining room, from the dining room to the kitchen, and none of my sentences had either head or tail. I'll confess now that all I was thinking of was how to be alone with Madame Olga later, even for a little while. So that I could say to her, "I can't go on; I don't know why I'm telling it to you, but I have to tell someone, I can't imagine even one more day. I don't know why I married and why I have children. I don't know why I worked for so long on an instrument that now has no value for anyone. Do you know that I burned all the blueprints for my gun-sight? That doesn't interest you, I know. Besides, I wanted to tell you something quite different. And I don't really know what. I'm at the end of my tether; we're all in a dead-end street, but you least of all, because you're going away from this graveyard full of live corpses. I'd like to go with you... I can't go on living like this!"

Then I began to wonder whether I'd find the courage to tell her I loved her, and whether it would be true if I said it. I looked at myself in the mirror, saw my old face and felt ashamed. Just then you frightened me terribly. You said a very short sentence, again in that colorless, indifferent voice, and I thought I heard:

"But you know that I'm not jealous!"

"What did you say?"

"That I'm not jealous!"

So I had heard right. For God's sake, is she a mind-reader? Or are we both going crazy?

"My Heavens, how did you come to that...?"

"But you're not listening to me at all! What are you thinking of?"

The question sounded more mocking than reproachful. The doorbell saved me; my chief had just arrived.

He was out of breath, flurried, loquacious, and he brought you a bouquet. I hardly knew him. His familiarity and inquisitiveness infuriated me. Without being asked to, he looked through our whole apartment. And might he light a cigar? You reproved me because I had cigarettes for our guests instead of cigars. What do I think about all the time, you asked.

"He's been so absent-minded of late, sir!"

I was angry. Why does she call him "sir"? I asked her not to...

He consoled you. He smokes only a certain brand of cigar, rather rare in Prague, and I would probably have had a lot of trouble to get them. And after all, aren't we all absent-minded these days, and it's no wonder, the politicians got us into a nice mess! But the most important thing is not to lose our heads!

"Just remember, my friend, don't lose your head!"

I thought to myself, is he so extraordinarily repulsive today, or is it me? I noticed that even you were not too pleased with him. And then—may he have a word alone with me, if madame will permit.

We sat down opposite each other in the library. He flicked off the ash from his cigar on the floor, although I conspicuously handed him an ash tray twice. He had an aperitif, and sniffed it a while before he drank it. I was sipping soda water.

"You are, my friend, almost unpleasantly ascetic!"

I listened absent-mindedly. From the neighboring room the voices of Madame Olga and my secretary came to us; they must have arrived at the same time. They brought presents for the girls. You said they shouldn't have done it, but at the same time you were exclaiming over the charm of the gifts.

"No, you shouldn't have bought that, you really shouldn't have! I'm angry at you—oh, how lovely it is!"

It upset me; in those seconds everything irritated me, and all at once I realized that I must do something extraordinary, something altogether out of the run of my usual life. Otherwise I should suffocate. I felt that I must at least run away from my life for a while, that I could no longer swallow its silt, that at least for the last time, before I rot, I had to get drunk on some thought, some passion or love, that I had to break something inside myself or about myself, storm, run up to a high place—and then perhaps leap to death. It is hard for me to describe my hunger for redemption, for the action which I could not imagine. Perhaps then I might have made up my mind to a deed which later would have been worth a headlong plunge, if in the midst of all my confused thoughts had not burned the dark, mysterious eyes of futility. If I had not been pursuing a phantom and madness, whose shadow in my face bore a resemblance to Madame Olga.

Mr. Schwartz talked as if he were talking against time. He said a great deal about one thing: he wants to have it clear! Is it true that I am not planning to finish my gun-sight? And do I realize that the factory which gave me the time and the means to do my work is to some extent part-owner of my idea? This is certainly no proper time for my caprices!

Under the onslaught of his unaccustomedly sharp words I quickly concentrated my thoughts. I said that I certainly did not agree with him.

"'I don't agree! I don't agree!' Those words seem to occur the most frequently in your dictionary! They're the heraldic words of the Czech language and have already caused trouble enough!"

What is the man babbling? Why is he so strange today? Is he drunk?

"I don't understand why you are blaming me for a fault which we share — that is, I believe that you are a Czech too."

"Look, my friend, this way we'll never come to any agreement. We are living in a revolutionary era, and we don't have much time. Give me your blueprints, finish your work, and there'll come a day when you won't be sorry you did!"

It hurt me and fatigued me to quarrel about a thing which had been decided long ago. My objections sounded sleepy.

"Sir, the Czechoslovak government no longer has any interest in my sight for anti-aircraft guns. And I shall neither give nor sell anything to the English or the French. Maybe later on, if they ever make up for what they have done. Please allow me to have my own tastes, at least."

He exploded, "Colleague, please, don't play the proud and capricious Edison!"

This hit a sensitive spot, probably because I was really proud of my invention. I threw down my last card, which I had no idea of even showing originally.

"Well, the day after Munich I burned all the blueprints."

He jumped up as if I had poured boiling water over him.

"Man, that is—that is—I don't know what to call it!"

I was distracted again. Madame Olga was just giving her future Paris address. In that instant my unfortunate thought was born. I would follow her! At least for two days! I must speak with her. After all, no one would ever find out about it.

"What did you say?"

"Nothing more, colleague."

And really Mr. Schwartz no longer had anything on his mind. He knew what to do now. Then we went in to supper. God knows how many big and little betrayals ripened while we ate! We spoke about books, the movies and maids. Madame Olga was pale, sad and quiet. She kept looking at me as if she were trying to decide whether I was to be depended on. She wanted something of me, there was no doubt of that. My chief swallowed great mouthfuls with ill-concealed rage. He kept looking at the clock, and always forgot where it hung. Lame Anna kept tying the torn thread of conversation with unbreakable determination and endurance. I kept thinking only that I would go to Paris, find Madame Olga, and tell her everything. Everything—and what was that? I had no idea. But the temptation of the first sin was swooningly alluring. And you, Hanichka? Were you then seeing more than I saw, or did you see nothing? Your eyes were neither angry nor horrified, only a little amazed. They glided from one to the other of us, and said to us gently: "Say it, don't be afraid, say it all!" If nothing else, then you must have realized how many secret plans there were in us, and how many opposing wills. And that as soon as we got up from the table there would be an end to the atmosphere in which somehow five people had managed to pretend to be friends.

When the group was leaving, my lame secretary whispered to me in the anteroom:

"Please don't go away to a foreign country now!"

"I don't understand you."

"You might never be able to return!"

I was not sure that I had heard right, and I didn't have time to ask just what she was getting at. And the next day I had forgotten all about it.

But later, when they brought me a ticket from the airline office, Anna recognized the envelope and guessed that I was getting ready to make a trip. She reached for both her canes, stood at her desk, and said, her teeth chattering:

"At least tell me where you are going to stay!"

She had never before spoken to me in this inquisitorial tone.

"For Heaven's sake, what does this mean?"

"You are going to Paris!"

I started with fright and anger. But when I saw tears on my secretary's cheeks I controlled myself and swallowed my rudeness.

"What's that you're saying? Anna, we have been the best of friends for eight years. Don't do anything…"

"I want to do nothing more than to be able to send word to you in case it's necessary. Promise me that you will stay in a hotel—perhaps the Glacière, Rue de la Glacière."

"Anna, I've had enough of this!"

She mumbled some incomprehensible words, trembled all over, while a stream of tears poured down her cheeks. All at once she became angry.

"You're blind, you'll kill yourself! I'd risk my head on it—he has reported you!"

"Are you crazy? Who's reported me? To whom? And why?"

"For that gun-sight… Please listen to me… Remember, Rue de la Glacière…"

I turned away, shrugged my shoulders and left the office.

4

WHEN A MAN is surrounded by solitude and hears nothing but the beating of his own heart, when all the mirrors of futility and vanity are unsilvered, when we are so close to death and its solicitous embrace that we see ourselves, our friends and our enemies through the reconciling mist of the grave—at such times we don't do much lying to ourselves about our errant footsteps. So it is no lie when I tell you that I never deserted you. I didn't leave you, Hanichka, to betray you, never to return to you. My case is quite different. I flew secretly from Prague to Paris just at the time when impotence was the heaviest cross of all of us. And I couldn't bear it any longer. I set out on a journey into emptiness. I went in search of a beggar's coin far away, never knowing that what I was seeking I could find only in myself—or nowhere. I wanted to tell someone that I loved her, and I wanted to hear someone say she loved me. In those days, millions of people were going astray just as I did. Words of love and hope melted on our lips, as soon as they were pronounced. The breath of eternity was gone from them because we had destroyed their validity. But there remained in us a hunger for what had been in the beginning, somewhere on the threshold of life, and our throats were parched with thirst after the fruits of those eternal words of which we had on our tongues only the dry and bitter husks. The more we spoke, the deeper was our silence. We suffered because we did not fight, and we went astray because we made detours around the difficult paths. Well then, what was really my fault? I did not want to believe the thing that was manifested to me; I did not want to seek protection in myself, in you and what was around us. I flew away to Paris and stumbled through her gaudy noisiness in search of a phantom which had to dissolve at the first touch.

Madame Olga and I were sitting in wicker chairs at a window of a spacious café which looked out on the Boulevard St. Michel. We were sipping some kind of sweet beverage, in the midst of the buzz of voices, mists of smoke and the smell of coffee and tea.

Madame Olga was not surprised when I found her. That woman never seemed to be surprised. She asked no questions. She listened. I told her that I had some work to do in Paris, but that I had really come on account of her. I told her that on the first day. We were almost constantly together. In the shops, in cafés, in the theater. Not once did she ask when I would finally tell her what I wanted of her. Her conversation was purely reportorial. "Look, that's a beautiful dress. Our porter is terribly funny. If it were warmer I'd order ice cream. I'm almost sure that I shall find no work in Paris. My friend advises me to leave for Brazil."

I felt that I could no longer put off my poor, only half-prepared monologue. And so, in that café with its view of the Boulevard St. Michel, I started, shyly and in a monotone: I know that I have not the slightest right to hope for her favor (I don't like that word, but I could find no more suitable one), I know that I am already an older man, that I have a wife and grown children, but still…

I stopped and started differently, this time sentimentally. Everything is falling to ruin around us, suddenly life lies before us bare and crude. I am terribly sad because I feel forsaken. I retired too much into solitude, and now I am becoming conscious of its killing breath. In vain I seek for people who might draw me out of it. My last hope is she herself, Madame Olga. I want nothing of her—only…

Again I was silent for a long time and then I jerked out timorously and unconvincingly: "I love you—for years now—I don't know how I will—without you…"

She stroked my hand, smiled, and whispered:

"I know!"

She waited a while to see if I still had anything in my heart, and then she spoke, soothingly and with a kind of melancholy resignation. My emotion swiftly changed to hesitation and then to amazement.

She said that she too was not as young as she once had been. She said that she respected me and that is usually more than love. She understood everything; long before her husband's death, marriage had begun to bore her also. Circumstances drove her out of Prague, she is completely alone, she has been depending on me secretly for a long time. She does not want me to break up my family, she wants very little and hopes that this will be enough for me too. I can take care of her and I shall find that she will be more than a good friend to me.

If I had expected anything, certainly *this* was not it. I caught my breath with the shock. I understood only that I could have her. That she was offering me something which I had never dared even to think about. Lustful joy fought in me with a feeling that resembled disillusion. The joy and temptation were stronger and, for a while, they cried down the ugly thought: Why, she is offering herself to you for money!

But this thought persevered. And Madame Olga tried to do nothing to silence it. She said that no matter what happened at home now, I should always be free and unhampered. I could come to Paris; I could find a home now and she could take care of it…

Everything around me started to waver; I stopped taking things in and understanding them. I wanted to be alone for a while. Blushing with embarrassment, I begged her permission to go away for a little while. I said that even in my boldest dreams I hadn't dared to hope… And for that reason now I was confused, so happily confused, yes, that I must be alone for a while. In the evening we should meet—this evening we should celebrate our—friendship, our new friendship!

I kissed her hand. And she said:

"You're a great child! Now go and meditate, but this evening I shall be waiting for you in the hotel. Oh, no! This evening I have something I can't get out of! But that doesn't matter. Come late! After eleven!"

I ran out of the café. For the first time since my youth my blood burned with a feeling like great joy or great enthusiasm. But it was neither the one nor the other. I was standing on the threshold of betrayal. Yes, that time I was not far from betraying you, Hanichka! The air, washed with recent rain, rushed into my lungs; all at once there was too much of it; my breath came faster and my heart beat harder; the air smelled of a drink which I could no longer remember and drifted lightly into all my senses with the rhythm of some long-forgotten love song. God, how strange a man feels in his heart when he is getting ready to betray! He looks around to see if anyone is following him, and all the chance passers-by who hardly notice him seem so pleasant, so kind, so wise. He rejoices because he is lost amongst thousands, because no one knows his intention, because he is unshackled, liberated, free, alone with his temptation.

People walked around mud puddles, they walked on tiptoe so comically, there was much more laughter in their talking than there was at home, the automobiles went faster than at home, the women seemed younger and the children livelier. "You're in Paris!" I said to myself, "you can dye your hair and no one will laugh at you, you can change your name, you can…"

I had not even realized that I was walking back and forth past the windows of the café which I had left a little while ago. Suddenly I saw Madame Olga. She was still sitting at the same table. And she looked as if she had turned to stone. Her hands were folded before her, her head was bowed toward her left shoulder, her lips were parted in a frozen smile. That is how I left her and that is how she remained. Startled, I watched her, not able to discern a single flicker of life in her rigidity. I sighed with relief when she finally moved in an abrupt gesture which tore her hands apart and lifted her head. As if she had been frightened, or as if death had touched her. But she stiffened again in a new position. But this time only for a little while. Before long she laid her hands palms up on the table and caught her drooping head. Her whole body was shaken by violent weeping.

I remember that I bared my head for no reason whatever. Then I fumbled through my pockets for a handkerchief to wipe my eyes. But they were dry. A policeman stepped up to me and asked me if I was looking for something. I handed him my passport, but he waved it away with a smile. He said that he had only wanted to help me because I looked very much at a loss. I assured him that he could not help me, turned on my heel, and walked away. It was drizzling. But

I didn't even notice the rain or the penetrating cold which constricted my breast and numbed my toes.

I walked and walked aimlessly through the swarming Paris streets. A deep melancholy shadowed my whole mood. A freezing dampness was on my skin and in my thoughts. Without feeling very upset, and without any great pain, I realized that I had gone astray. That I had left my home, my wife and my children, that I had unwillingly inspired a strange woman to make an ugly plan which made her cry as soon as she had made it known, that we should never meet again and never see each other again, that I should think for a long time about the temptation to betrayal, my own awkwardness and foolishness, and that my unnavigable life would continue to flow lazily on in its old channel. I should return home that very day, tomorrow at the latest.

The rain washed my temples and showed me the world through a veil of fine tears. Only a little while ago I had had the fire of youth within me, and people and things had seemed wonderfully new and good. Now again the worm of futile indifference gnawed at my brain and heart, people were repulsive, banal, uncouth, and things were useless, ugly and bad. Where had the magic spark of hope vanished? My God, where had all the potent beauty and strength of youth vanished, which had been brought back to me only a little while ago by the temptation to betray? The dripping of the rain and the light swirling of smells, voices and sounds made a lullaby for my thoughts. I dreamed with my eyes open. All at once the wide boulevards were my first roads into life, the still life of window displays was the hiding place of childish wealth, the playful noise of marketplaces was the rhythm of long-ago games, the fantastic grouping of buildings was the castles-in-the-air of my first daring plans. Once again the city of cities bewitched one of a million fools for a little while. That city of light rustlings, of sweetly secret speech, of blue grayness, of lovers' perfumes, of madcap laughter and disguises of magicians and adventurers. Again one of a million simpletons wandered through Paris, finding in the charming disarray of her allegorical little shops the treasures of childhood, and recognizing in the fleeting glances of her bleached golden blondes the beauties of youth, and in the faces of her soldiers, bakers and chauffeurs, comrades from the fantastic tales of dreams long ago turned to dust. As I staggered through Paris I wandered through Christmas Eves, through days of great fairs, through the twilight of summer vacations when I was a schoolboy, through daybreaks with fires on the hillsides, through the chocolate afternoons of birthday celebrations!

Where had the joy of those days vanished? The winds had carried it off and the rains had washed it away. With what had I paid for it then? With courage, faith and prayer. That all died. With what could I pay for it today?

For a while I came back to myself. I remembered my home, the way back, and my heart ached. It ached so that I groaned. But in that second I understood. I still had something with which I could pay: pain and suffering. Why, I had never really suffered before!

But even then—just as often before—revulsion drove away the spark of truth. I started to feel sorry for myself. I wasn't suffering? I avoided pain? I answered myself with a wicked laugh and started to lie to myself that I was the unhappiest of the unhappy, an outcast and a martyr.

And then the evening came and the rain stopped. The light-footed mass threw itself toward the colored lights and the rockets of laughter, shrieks and dance music that burst out of cafés, saloons and bars. The eternal stream of boisterous festivity, invincible merriment and unconcealed libertinism seemed to be threatened by nothing. It swept along with it everything living or lifeless. Only I stood somehow apart—I, then a drenched policeman at the crossing, and finally a crippled beggar under the lantern of a dubious hotel. I gave him a few francs. He seemed neither surprised nor touched. I had the wish to plunge headlong into that frothy maelstrom of lights, sounds, human smells and bleating voluptuousness.

"Come and have a drink with me," I said to the cripple with tense affability. He did not answer. Perhaps he was deaf. Good, at least my head wouldn't ache tomorrow! I don't even know how to drink!

It happened right after I left the cripple. Somewhere ahead of me an invisible newsboy shouted twice, "Extra! Extra!" A group of excited people came running out of the dubious hotel. Their argument, or their loud conversation, flowed together into an incomprehensible buzzing, out of which I could only catch a resounding insult to "dirty foreigners." A woman's voice shrilled the insult. Just then a powerful workman ran into me. He reeked of beer. He squeezed my shoulders gently, as if in apology, and then he said confidentially, "This looks like general mobilization!" Before I could ask what had happened, he was gone. I looked around, but I could not see or hear any more extraordinary things. The rather pert, rather lazy nocturnal stream really seemed to be threatened by nothing. Only an unusual number of pedestrians read newspapers as they walked. I still remember that fate had chosen an unshaven youth with a cigarette pasted in the left corner of his mouth to reveal the truth to me. That young man went along like a blind man or a somnambulist; only God knows how it was that he neither stumbled nor collided with other pedestrians. As he walked he peered into an outspread newspaper which he held in his stiff hands far from his face. He must have been far-sighted. I went past him several times, looking at his newspaper in vain. I did not succeed in reading anything in it. And again a newsboy not far away cried, "Extra!" Damn, where was he shouting? Where were all these people buying their papers? Wasn't there a newsstand anywhere?

"Pardon me, sir," I addressed the young man, "could you tell me what has happened?"

He stared at me, laughed, spat skillfully without removing his cigarette from his mouth, and said:

"I don't know; what could have happened? I'm studying a crossword puzzle, *hein*? On the way home I always play with it a little, but I don't really solve it until I'm home in bed, *hein*? Just a minute, maybe you know the name of the most famous English king in the sixteenth century? It's—one, two, three—five letters—no, a moment… Oh, yes, you think that something has happened, so let's just look at the front page, *hein*? Aha, here it is!"

I read: THE END OF CZECHOSLOVAKIA. In smaller letters I read a few words about the journey of the Czechoslovak President to Berlin and about the German regiments in Moravská Ostrava.

"Thank you!" I jerked out. "Good night!" and I offered my hand to the young man. He thought that I was either drunk or crazy, and he was amused. He willingly clasped my right hand. "Good night, *mon petit bonhomme*," he laughed rudely and walked off. So did I.

I tried to think. From Ostrava to Prague is about—how many kilometers? Who could have been the most famous English king in the sixteenth century? The end of Czechoslovakia! That means… To jump into the Seine? Oh, not yet! Now I shall never see Madame Olga again, and I shall never even think of her any more. Of course, I must go back. By now the Germans may be in Prague. Where will they spend the night? In the schools and churches, naturally.

Maybe they will spare the cemeteries. Besides, what would they be doing in cemeteries? The end of Czechoslovakia! My gun-sight… Anna wanted… No, only no nonsense! Suicide is cowardice, if you please! My father said it and Professor Marek said it and once Marta repeated it after me, she said it to Johanna. God, God, have mercy! Anna wanted me to stay at the Hotel Glacière. "Taxi! Taxi!" I'm lucky; it stopped. "Rue de la Glacière!" Keep calm, friend, it's indispensable, that calm! The most important thing is not to lose your head. Remember, friend, not to lose your head! How many people may have gone insane in this instant? Let's say, five thousand. They will probably spare the cemeteries. We're here already? Impossible!

The driver took the bill I handed him without taking his eyes off me. "How can I change this for you? Do you think I steal?"

"Keep the change!"

"*Merci, Monsieur, merci beaucoup, cher monsieur!* Are you an American? And if you don't mind—would you have—do you have a handkerchief? If you don't, then at least wipe your face with your sleeve! You look terrible! Did someone die?"

"My whole family!"

"*Zut alors!* An accident?"

"Yes."

"Have a cognac. That's good for the nerves."

"You're right. A cognac. Thank you."

And once more I shook hands with a stranger.

5

W E PURSUED the crumbs of life, while our whole life was disintegrating. I feel, Hanichka, that you must have lived through something very similar. In an instant I aged by ten years and all the former play with love, petty worries and still pettier sufferings were far away in hell. I could hardly recall the focus of yesterday's thoughts. It was as if I had met Madame Olga for the last time years ago, and as if I had been a widower for a long time. Besides, my memories of those days in Paris are not at all clear. The very first night I wrote you a long letter. I don't know what I said in it; I tore it up.

I stayed a week in the Hotel Glacière waiting for news from Anna. I spent most of the time in my room; I sat on the bed and stared into space. I ate only once or twice a day. Whenever I found myself out in the street I felt horrified that the world had not swerved from its orbit, that people dressed as they did before, that they ate, drank, laughed, pretended to work and really worked, just as if nothing had happened. But then, I myself could scarcely understand all that had happened, why the blood drained from my face whenever I whispered to myself: these shoes I still bought in Prague, there and there, then and then. Hanna gave me this necktie last Christmas. Last Christmas! Why last? And then I had a quarrel with the manager.

"You're a Czechoslovak, aren't you, sir?" he asked me, digging in his ear with his penholder.

"Yes!"

"Hm, a sad story! But why, in the devil's name, didn't you fight?"

I roared, frightening myself with my own voice, that he was an idiot, and he, quite calmly and without removing the penholder from his ear, invited me to leave his hotel by evening.

By good luck a letter from Anna came before evening. It was mailed in Switzerland. Anna explained that Engineer Smetana was taking the letter from Prague to Berne, that he was dependable and would probably send it on to me in Paris at once. It was a love letter, only half-intelligible, and in parts completely hysterical. She wrote that she loved me. That everything was her fault because jealousy had kept her from speaking clearly in time. She knew that I had followed Madame Olga to Paris. How could I do anything like that to my wife, and to her, Anna, and to all the people who had faith in me? I sealed my own fate by following that path. Is it a punishment? Oh, that would be too cruel a punishment! She wrote that Mr. Schwartz was a traitor, that he had informed the Germans about my gun-sight long ago, the Germans had been looking for me ever since the first day of the occupation, they had issued a warrant for my arrest, and if they already knew that I was in Paris, no one would ever be able to convince them that I had not given the blueprints for my gun-sight to the French. I could not and I dared not return; they would torture me to death. I could not even imagine, she said, how the Germans were acting, how wildly they were making arrests, without plans, without rhyme or reason. Perhaps it was her fault, perhaps my own, perhaps everyone's, because each one of us loved someone and something that it was forbidden for us to love. (Anna underscored this sentence.) May I forgive her, she wrote, she would pray for me and I should never forget my unhappy country.

So Anna was in love with me! But the revelation scarcely penetrated my thoughts. I didn't understand people as they were yesterday. I didn't understand my own recent experiences and their motives. It was as if I were suddenly being called upon to play a strange role. But still Anna's letter did not depress me; quite the contrary.

As soon as I finished reading it I began to persuade myself that Providence had sent me to France. It seemed to me that I was confronted with a great mission, that I must forget everything that had been and was, and give my invention to the French. That was the only way I could redeem myself, you, Hanichka, and my country; that was the only way to do penance for my real and imagined sins.

I was imbued with vainglory. I worked night and day at my plans and then wandered from office to office, from person to person… ah, let us pass over as quickly as possible the most painful chapter of my life! The French considered my invention, for which I had become an outlaw, an unnecessary, luxurious plaything, and myself a crackpot. The comedy approached its climax.

Added to everything else, my money was running low, and French government offices demanded more and more documents, and anyone who could not afford to give bribes had to run around for days on end. I moved from hotel to hotel, from more expensive ones to cheaper ones, and at last I was living on the outskirts of town in a dirty little attic room. I grew a beard, and my hair got so long that it covered my collar. I had one frayed suit and a little underwear.

And then war broke out and a Czechoslovak army formed in France. I reported without enthusiasm, but they rejected me: they said that they would not win the war with men of my age. But even then I felt no anger, no pity, no despair, only a kind of melancholy defiance. Something like pride. Several times I caught myself talking to myself and threatening someone: only wait! Just you wait! I hadn't worked for months and I didn't even long for work. Sometimes I met people I knew from home, poor, terrified refugees as well as wealthy emigrés, who were probably going to cross the ocean. But no one recognized me. I myself approached no more than five of my countrymen. I was not lonely for company. They wrung their hands over me, they offered me help, and, when I refused it, suspicious glances stole into their exchanges with me.

One day, I was standing on the banks of the Seine aimlessly staring into the water. I felt a man walking past me and watching me. I was already reaching for my papers, sure that it was a policeman, but I was too lazy to turn around.

"Would you do me a small favor, sir?" someone right behind me asked. It seemed to me that the voice had a mocking sound. I answered without moving:

"Not gladly! Besides, you will be disappointed, for my papers are in perfect order."

"I don't want any papers," the mocker spoke again. "Now that you have spoken, I beg you even more urgently for a small favor which is scarcely worth speaking about: please turn around!"

I obeyed. The mocker was a tall, slim dandy of about forty-five, bald, clean-shaven, long-handed, long-fingered, and he smoked a pipe. We looked at each other closely. He twisted his mouth in a disagreeable smile which matched perfectly the stinging tone of his voice, and I trembled a little. He did not recognize me, but I recognized him.

"That's all, thank you. I made a mistake. Forgive me, sir, for interrupting your philosophizing," the tall man grimaced and nodded good-bye to me.

"Wait!" I called to him quietly.

He stopped and measured me from head to foot. I considered whether or not to make myself known to him.

And I became upset, as I always did in those days when it happened, as it did once in a while, that by chance I stood face to face in a Paris street with some man I once knew.

"You made no mistake," I stammered at last. "You are Dr. Aubin, aren't you?"

I can't remember any more, Hanichka, if I ever told you about him. Many years ago Dr. Pacak introduced him to me in Prague. At one time they had studied together at the Sorbonne and at the time I met Aubin he had just stopped in Prague on his way to the doctors' congress in Moscow, to see his old friend. He interrupted his journey to Russia only for a few days, but of those three or four days we used to see each other every evening, for of all Pacak's friends I was the only one who could speak French well. He made no very great impression on me and so it's very likely that I mentioned him to you only in passing, if I ever spoke of him to you at all. He was too sarcastic for my taste, and his pipe, which was always going out, and his really unpleasant grimaces (especially the way he constantly twisted his mouth, puckered his lips, pushed out and pulled back his chin) repelled rather than attracted me. But he was a type that you remember forever, even after only one conversation.

That time, when we met by chance on the banks of the Seine, he was not repulsive to me. In contrast to the several people whom I did not know very well, to whom I had allowed myself to be made known since I was in Paris, he did not make the sign of the cross over me, and he did not shriek, "Man alive, what has happened to you!" and he did not annoy me with intrusive questions. Just as if my beard and sorry appearance did not surprise him in the least, and as if it were only to be expected that he should meet me in Paris. He showed his teeth and gripped my hand.

"I only guessed it was you from your back and shoulders. When you spoke I would have wagered my neck that I had guessed right. But then your face confused me again. How are you getting along? Do you know anything about Dr. Pacak? Probably not. But then, that one! Nothing will happen to him, he's a *débrouillard*, he knows how to handle any situation. Come along with me for a cup of coffee! I'll put cognac in mine and you'll put cream in yours—you see, I even remember that you're a teetotaler!"

I went. First for coffee and later for supper. I kept almost entirely silent; he spoke for me, although he had never been talkative. He recalled Prague, the National Theater, our coffee houses and restaurants, Dr. Pacak and the little stories about him. He referred to the occupation several times, but his voice never broke and he never let it be colored by any sentimental sighs. He spoke of what had happened with utter cynicism.

"That's how it is when someone depends on France! If I had been you people, I should have sooner bet on Luxembourg! They have a Grand Duchess there and a person can come to a much better understanding with a woman than with our Radical Socialist politicians. I read that right after Munich the pictures of the presidents vanished from your walls. In your place I should have hung Daladier and Chamberlain on the wall. And what do you think, have the Germans drunk up all the Pilsner beer yet? Believe me, it's the only thing I envy them, oh, yes, and those Prague sausages. I'll never forget them as long as I live!"

I was fit to listen patiently only to such light banter. At times I even smiled. But I had got so out of the habit of smiling that it hurt me. I noticed how Aubin was forcing himself with all his might to carry on this empty conversation and I finally decided to help him out.

"And you, doctor, aren't you interested in how I got to Paris, and why I look like a tramp?"

"Upon my word, no, *mon vieux*! That is what my lady patients don't like about me—that I am not at all curious about their boudoir histories, which, according to them, have a direct bearing, let us say, on inflammation of the middle ear. They hold that against me—that, and then my freedom and bachelorhood."

"But I don't want to say that I came here for some kind of boudoir affair." As I said that sentence I sweated a little, because I remembered Madame Olga and her proposal.

"If it will relieve you, comrade, make your confession, but please bear in mind that I did not urge you to confess."

I told him my story briefly. I boiled it down to a melodramatic episode, in which the chief parts, besides my own, were played by the villain Schwartz and good Anna, and whose kernel was my sight for anti-aircraft guns. When I came to the place in my story where I told about my futile attempts to gain the attention of the French Ministry of War for my invention, he burst out into such a loud and hearty laugh that he choked. That spoiled my mood and I became silent again.

"But, man, that's a wonderful farce! Excuse me, if it makes me hold my sides! So the Germans want to arrest you because in their judgment our people got an epoch-making invention from you. And our people meantime sent you packing with your invention. In order not to starve in some concentration camp at home, you stayed in sweet France, where they fed you so well that you could disguise yourself as a rail without any trouble. I ask you, who wouldn't laugh? Doesn't it seem funny to you?"

"Certainly not!"

"You're a strange creature. Everything seems too tragic to you. To me again nothing seems tragic. Not even that France will lose this war. Whether with your wonderful gun-sight or without it. Listen here, my friend, what about coming to stay with me in the country? You probably don't know Normandy anyhow. I have a car near here, and if you'll just wait for me an hour—I have a few little things to take care of here—I'll come back for you, load you into my auto with your baggage, if you have any, and we'll be home in three hours. I don't want to urge you, but you'd be doing me a great service if you came with me. I get terribly bored out there in my little nest in the country. I've been looking for an agreeable sacrifice for some time who might accept my invitation. How about it? Well, I think you'll take pity on me and come along!"

He didn't have to coax me much. I went and stayed with him for two whole weeks. All around his villa, which stood on a low slope, stretched meadows of winter gray. From the windows, which, for some unknown reason, the builder had set unusually high up from the floor, could be seen a winding brook, rocks, willow-brakes and the tangled threads of paths. The villa, in a group of four flimsy houses, stood a little apart from the country town, huddled in a deep hollow.

Immediately after my arrival I was seized with exhaustion, which was not at all unpleasant to me. I don't remember the first days very well, because for the most part I slept through them. When I finally came to myself out of that swooning drowsiness, I felt unusually refreshed. Dr. Aubin looked me over front and back, as if I were a tailor's mannequin on whom he was getting ready to drape a new outfit.

"I'd shave off those whiskers," he said expertly, "and then I'd see how some of George's suits would look on me. George was my oldest cousin, about your build, but God forbid that I should want to compare you with him. He went crazy, that is, and took it into his head that he would live with no one but a doctor. I love the notions of madmen, and so I took him into my home. Every day we had extraordinarily interesting conversations—I have them recorded somewhere. They were exactly like the jargon of our newspapermen today. He also claimed that if war broke out we would be able to stand up to Germany, Italy and maybe even to Russia. But then he began to rave. I put him in fetters and locked him in the cellar. I have a little laboratory down there, with rats, guinea pigs and rabbits; I raised them for experiments to which my colleagues at congresses refuse to attach any scientific weight. Oh, yes, to return to my cousin... I fed him at the same time that I fed my animals and I unfettered him whenever he calmed down. Then he would tell perfectly charming stories. I always had the feeling that I was sitting in some European parliament listening to the exposé of the foreign minister. Well, it was progressive paralysis. He didn't last long. I hope that this joyless narrative will not give you an antipathy to my cousin's suits and underwear."

But both the suits and underwear were obviously brand new. I acted as if I believed the story about the cousin. I dared not thank him too much. Words of thanks were the only words which threw Dr. Aubin into embarrassment and bad humor.

He had many patients, and his hands were full. He prepared our meals himself. He was an excellent cook and confided his recipes to me in the passionate voice of a man who is betraying an extraordinary secret. An old charwoman came to the little villa every day. Otherwise Aubin lived all alone; aside from his patients no one ever visited him.

I helped him in the kitchen, I fed his animals in the cellar, I took care of his garden and read the novels in his library, whose volumes of both poetry and prose represented such a fantastic potpourri that no matter how hard you tried it would be impossible to build up an idea of the taste and preference of the owner. And we took long walks. From the realms of mist I returned to life, and with life my memories came back to me. I thought about home, about you, about my birthplace, and, most of all, about the time of courage and faith. Thoughts of you, of the children, of Prague and my friends, saddened me; but memories from the heroic times of my life filled me with an intoxicating excitement. "Now it is just like the time," I said to myself, "when I first ran away from home into the forest. My heart beat just as fast. Won't I get lost? Will I find the way back? I wonder what's hiding behind that log? Oh, what moved in that brush? A ghost? A nymph?" Yes, it was just the same as it was then!

Once Dr. Aubin went away to Paris for a whole week. The evening of his return he said to me, very casually:

"Before I forget—I met Paul Villard. You've heard of him? He has a big munitions plant near Paris. He was mad as hops because they've taken his best engineer into the army and for some mysterious reason no one seems to be able to get his release. I mentioned you to him. He all but kissed me. He wants to meet you; he says he can get you a work permit. What do you think of it?"

And I kept right on pretending that I did not see through my host; that was the only way to get along with him.

"I'm amazed! Why, your friend knows nothing at all about me! Nothing about me personally, nothing about my former work, how then…?"

"He knows everything! I told him an earful! What I didn't know, I made up. By the way, did the rats eat while I was gone? Yesterday nothing seemed to appeal to them. Well, look, Wednesday after office hours I have to go to Paris again. Come along and look Mr. Villard over!"

To cut a long story short, he succeeded in transforming me into a man of whom it is possible to say that he is a useful member of society. He found work for me. I lived in Paris again, I lived in a respectable hotel, I was particular about my appearance and didn't give myself much time for sad thoughts. We didn't see each other for a long time, and we wrote very seldom.

Now I was patient. I had the feeling that I was living in the waiting room of a railroad station. The echo of events came to me like the signal to board the train, and I felt that everyone was waiting with me for a train that was late. After all there was a war—a war for the way back. For a return from that dog's life. A war for our redemption. Or for something else? I drove away all my doubts with work.

But one day they stood before me in a long column and couldn't be driven away. The Germans attacked France and France was crumbling. Fear began to gnaw at the bones of Paris, and probably at the bones of all Europe. The terror of doomsday was suddenly burned into the eyes of millions.

Everyone sought an alibi, everyone in my imaginary waiting room crowded to an exit—and there was none. Even knives flashed in the crowd. Save yourself, if you can! Blood bonds were rent, the godless started to pray and the godly started to steal and to betray. Paris was drained empty. Day and night the pavement trembled under the cars of wanderers journeying into emptiness. Terror seized me too, not so much of death, nor of the Germans, nor of torture, but of myself. How would I stand the unimaginable test?

And the pavement thundered and thundered in augury of the tribunal with the trumpeters of death. Remnants of ruined homes, piled on the roofs of cars, slithered down blind alleys. And from mouth to mouth flew the story that armed monsters were dropping from the clouds. A terrified whisper became the new rhythm of Paris. No one recognized the countless costumes of betrayal, whose breath you felt from the mouths of strangers and of friends.

Then they arrested me, locked me up and beat me. But I didn't suffer too much; you see, self-confidence and dignity had left me long ago, and we need them if we are to consider ourselves mature people. For a long time I had regarded myself as a naughty boy whom almost anyone might make stay after school, or whip. To this very day I don't know why it all happened. Possibly the French arrested all foreigners. And why did they beat me? The guardians of safety all over the world are convinced that it is necessary to beat prisoners. Just so. Out of tradition and for all emergencies.

My beard grew again, and again I smelled of filth and sweat. One morning they let me go and advised me to take to my heels if what I had told them was really true, because the Germans would be in Paris in no time.

I saw the sun again and I was free. But how strangely the sun shone then and how grotesque my freedom was! I kept thinking of the rabbit which farmers catch in their hands in the circle hunt. They let him go so that they can shoot him in flight, as huntsman's honor demands. In those few seconds before death is the rabbit free? Does he see the sun? Does he think of his hutch? Of sweet-scented clover? No, I did not see people around me, only rabbits, running a race with the wind. I started to run too. And it was a dual flight, outward and inward. That frantic rabbit's fleeing was in the blood, in the mind, in the heart. Otherwise I reeled rather than ran. Between trucks, automobiles, buggies and human scarecrows. As if the whole world were moving. And the countryside lost its features; everywhere it was the same, dark gray with terrified pilgrims and their poor burdens. I walked until I was exhausted, then someone took me part of the way on a motorcycle, then I rode on a wagon, and then I walked again.

At last I found the one I was looking for. Aubin stood in the doorway of his villa; he was smoking his pipe and twisting his mouth into a new kind of grimace. We didn't greet each other. For a while we looked at each other steadily, saying with our eyes what it was not possible to say with our lips. "Well, hurry up!" he finally burst out, and pulled me into the hall. It seems to me that he rubbed my arms and body for a while, as if he wanted to warm me up. His voice did not change.

"It's about time you came! An unusual diversion is waiting for us. You will stay with me. I've already put my darlings to death, naturally, on account of you! Instead of cages full of rats, guinea pigs and rabbits, I now have a nice iron bed in the basement. I'll hide you, I'll keep you hidden through the whole war! Well, man, smile a little! Don't you have any feeling at all for dangerous games? I'm so glad that I won't be alone. You mustn't go out, not even make a step out of doors, that's understood, but I'll never lock the door. You'd go crazy and act like my dead George. You must train your will, you must say, 'I know that I can go out into the light whenever I want to; all I have to do is turn the knob, but I won't do it.' Isn't that delightful? Come along now, we'll look over your new bedroom. Unfortunately, there's no stove in it. I had it taken out some time ago and now of course I can't have it reinstalled. It might attract attention. If you could only know how this wonderful idea entrances me, you'd be in the best of moods out of friendship! I adore the eccentric! I haven't felt so good in a long time as I do today! And now I have not the slightest intention of respecting your solid principles. Today you too are going to put cognac in your coffee instead of cream. No sneaking out of it, *à la guerre comme à la guerre*! And come along!"

6

I N THE FIRST DAYS one thought overshadowed all the others: the Germans are here already! Over me and around me! German soldiers. German police—in uniform and in civilian dress. If only I had seen some German uniforms before then, and if I had only seen some German regiments marching past, my anxiety would have either been less or different, less hideous. There is nothing worse than the fear of unimaginable people, things or events.

I felt safest in bed, bundled up in the covers, with a pillow wrapped around my head. But it was necessary to walk around too, stretch my legs, get washed and somehow keep myself occupied. Every rustle strained my nerves. In a thousand and one pictures I imagined myself: how they discover me, how they throw themselves upon me, how I succumb, how I moan and stretch out my clasped hands to them. I had no appetite; in those days I lived on fear. Dr. Aubin always dispelled it a little. He came to me like a ghost, on tiptoe and in the dark, but on his way downstairs he softly whistled a popular Parisian tune, so that I would know who was coming. He knew the cellar so well that he needed no light. He brought food, books, newspapers and often his radio. He whispered, and because the color of his voice was lost in the whisper, and because I could not see his face (he always came around midnight and from the very beginning until today he never struck a match) there were very few signs by which I could recognize him.

"They aren't even as terrible as people say they are, but they are more stupid than I had any idea they would be. Don't be frightened, but one of them lives right above you. An officer. He is interested in music and in André Gide, and I am sure he doesn't wear a monocle just to annoy me. He says he will stay with me for a week yet. I think that the unlocked door was an excellent idea. Tell me yourself, isn't it a relief to know that you are really free?"

Out of gratitude I assured him that it was a great relief. But the exact opposite was true. Especially ever since the day when someone came down the steps not whistling, into the neighboring room in the cellar, where, as far as I could remember, coal and garden tools were kept, half opened the door and looked toward me. My heart stopped beating. In the hole where I lived it was thick twilight even during the day; I became so accustomed to it before long that I could even read there. I pressed myself against the wall. The person who half opened the door did not enter, but the head, whose silhouette I could see, did not belong to Aubin. It would be hard to imagine my horror, which lengthened seconds into eternity. The nose was missing on the head of that intruder, or at least so it seemed to me. When the door quietly closed again, I couldn't move for a while, my whole body was turned to wood. Without a doubt that noseless man belonged amongst those unimaginable monsters which threatened me. I realized that I would be unable to defend myself if someone discovered me. I should grow numb confronted by a face which most certainly would not even be human.

It took me a long time to calm down. When the doctor visited me again I asked him if he had not seen amongst the Germans in the village one whose nose was missing. He laughed in an embarrassed way and did not answer for a while. I thought to myself: he is convinced that I have started to go mad! And I said very loudly: "That is to say I had a terribly real dream!"

"For God's sake, talk quietly!"

I was terrified again. This was not Aubin; he would never admonish me so angrily. Who was it then who came to me? We were quiet for a long time. I rubbed my temples. My breath wheezed. Then I asked, as if I were begging for mercy:

"Just tell me, doctor, quite honestly, what you are thinking now!"

"You worry me. But then, I was ready for it; every game has its candle."

That sounded like Aubin again. The vise which crushed my chest eased, and there was no whistling and rattling when I breathed. But something in my whispering kept crying beggingly.

"What will you do if I go crazy on you?"

"You won't go crazy!"

"But if I should?"

"Then we'll put on an act together that'll be worth it, to crown the madness we share. Look, there is no situation which I would not find amusing. I am incurably inquisitive, of course only about myself, and that is because no one ever taught us what to do in bizarre circumstances. I am sure that my curiosity will make me feel interested and entertained even on my deathbed. By the way: the Germans are beginning to carry on in rather an ugly way. There's a little shooting at night. They won't listen to reason and neither will we. What do you find lacking as far as you're concerned?"

"Lacking? Probably courage. Frankly, I'm afraid. And my fear makes me suffer hallucinations."

"You saw a German without a nose?"

"Yes, there in the doorway."

"You're lucky. I have to pay good money to see American films if I want the chills to chase each other up and down my back. Look here, learn to look at everything as if it were a thrilling play which does not concern you and which will end soon!"

"I'd like to learn how to do that."

"That means being prepared for death. Understand me, until death itself comes, everything is really only a play.

Damn it, we had miserable teachers; they never taught us the most important wisdom of all."

I asked humbly, like a child:

"And what should I do with my time?"

"Remember things, live again some times gone by. And when you live yourself into them, look over this resurrected time carefully and wisely. Pretend you are Marcel Proust. You never read him? Shame on you! Neither did I!"

He succeeded in bringing a smile to my lips.

"Thank you; I'll try to follow your advice."

"No, you won't go crazy! Well—if you do, no misfortune. And chin up, I say. I'd never dream of warning you, but you have to get hold of yourself or some day you'll be ashamed of yourself. That's usually an ugly feeling. And believe me that you have nothing to complain of. Many people who seem perfectly free and independent are a thousand times worse off today than you are. *Mon vieux*, those Germans are strange people after all; now that I know them a little better, I know absolutely certainly that our war with them will turn out a little better than I thought it would at the beginning. They aren't fighting against people but against nature. Do you remember from your school days the pampered, cruel and at the same time, cowardly prize-winners? That is what the Germans make me remember. Educated dunces, proud as the devil, silence annoys them the most, perhaps they sense that—even though by some mad chance they might occupy the whole world—in the end they will perish from the great silence of all the space into which they have fallen. And do you know, I even think that most likely they would spare you if you fell into their hands. They would forgive you that gun-sight; you aren't the type on which they like to vent their anger. That vexes me a little; it takes away from the dramatic quality of our story."

Nothing put me back on my feet like Aubin's biting words. They had the effect of making me feel a little ashamed of myself, and so getting back a little of my courage.

Time passed and a period of real want came upon us. There was not enough food and it was cold. But the greater my physical suffering the more easily my thoughts freed themselves from the world around me. Newspapers, radio broadcasts and Aubin's stories came to me from astronomical distances. My waking mingled with my dreaming. I succeeded in transporting myself into the past and living again my boyhood and youth, the period of my betrothal, my first journey into a foreign country, and again the twilight years of my childhood, a time woven of the hair of my nurses and the dark-brightness of firefly-lighted nights. I occupied myself with a spiritual game. I said to myself: today is Thursday, you are twelve years old, you get up at six o'clock in the morning so that you can catch the school train. Your first subject is natural history, the second, religion, then mathematics—oh, before class you still have to write out your assignment! And you've done nothing at all for German! You'll recite the vocabulary in the train.

I lived that whole day again, from breakfast through my last class period. I learned words, wrote my exercises, sent notes under the desk to my schoolmates, made fun of the teachers and during recess drew insulting pictures on an imaginary blackboard. Then I had lunch with Aunt Lucy, quarreled with my cousin over dessert, went for a walk, stopped at the bookstore of Mr. Bilek and bought myself the novel *The Secret Island*. At four o'clock in the afternoon I went to the station; on the way I discovered that I had left my pass in school and argued with myself whether to buy a ticket or ride home on the rods, like the bolder boys did in such emergencies. I decided in favor of the ticket, bought it with a heavy heart and then devoured the first pages of Verne's novel in the waiting room.

My memories and my visions were like blocks which I could use to build infinite structures. Day and night I constructed the past and the future. The future shrank to that picture of a return which I described to you, Hanichka, at the very beginning, and the past was a shoreless space with well-trodden paths leading to the harvests of love. I followed them again and this time I did not get lost. Led by the hands of my parents, my brothers and sisters, my nurses, my schoolmates and you, I got to the place, so happy and so enchanted, which I had never before reached. Into the far distances of peace, ruffled by a blue wind, broken by the song of a lark and the whistle of a tramp. Into the white snow storms in the streets of my native town, where displays in the windows of confectioneries and toy-shops reflected the ardor of the wide-open eyes of little children, where an angel and St. Nicholas led a horned devil on a chain to the delight, laughter and the first anxiety of the youngsters. Into the darkened closets with a skeleton and stuffed beasts, where the hearts of boys burn with longing to follow the crusading, honor-driven knights. Into mirror-lined ballrooms, where wings sprout on the girls' shoulders and where heavenly music comes down in a whirling vertigo. I saw all the roads which lead to the springs of life, all the roads blazed by love, those roads of children, of lovers and God's adventurers. Oh, Hanichka, how wonderful, sweet, wise and good life is, when it is seen out of emptiness! How sublime life is for the man betrothed to death!

A strange thing! During all these inner upheavals from the time of that illusive night when we went out to the country for the last summer, until today, when I may leave my cave any minute, I have had to return again and again to the dawn of my own life. The time of my childhood came back to me first when I dreamed of the little home of Mr. Andrejs and of the onslaught of ruin whose secret name is Karutmon. Then again when I went away from weeping Madame Olga and wandered through the streets of Paris. But it came back the most often during my captivity.

By the hour I struggled through a primeval forest of shadows in pursuit of a little circle of light; I heard the voice of a sunny morning and of a hidden spring. I was seeking the way to treasures, I was seeking it with the heart of a child, with the eyes of a child and the faith of a child. Yes, the key to the secret lies only in childhood, only in childhood is it possible to find the way to salvation. On its meadow-fresh plains, amongst flowers and bees, love slumbers, stripped of the clothes of passion. In its fields sings the siren of courage. In its colored shards, in the fires kindled by its little herds, in the songs of its birds, gladness laughs. In its dwellings God still lives and from its wells you can draw living water.

But there came days and nights when I did not have the strength to stumble back to the borders of that heavenly garden. I could not visualize our kitchen, the cupboards and the stove with its chipped pots, the tuneless, one-fingered playing on my sister's piano, the slanting columns of golden dust in our room in the country school. And I could not manage to tear from the past a piece of those bright times and hold its bewitching image before my mind's eye. Today I do not believe that I saw and understood reality in those bad moments. Reality is not a closed-up today without any path leading back to the past and without roads to the future. Reality is not only the truth of one moment. Reality is a stream of times past, present and future, the comradeship of people dead, living and still to be born; it is memory, will and dream, birth and death and then resurrection.

It was just then, when I was most blind that I became aware that I was imprisoned, that through the barred window, set in a deep recess, I could see nothing but a strip of sandy soil, and no sky at all. That my window was no window, that the half-soldered-up hole along the pipe by the chimney, taking the place of a window for me, gave me a view of only a sliver of free space, along which a human being passed only once in many days.

I saw so few faces! And I never once saw the face of a friend from the day I crossed the threshold of my burrow as a prisoner. In times of desperation I devoured the newspapers, begged invisible Aubin to let us listen oftener to the radio. In the daytime I watched at the pathetic opening into the world, asked myself and Aubin if I couldn't manage to escape somehow, after all. To the ocean, to England or to Switzerland, to Spain and then to Portugal and across the ocean. And when Aubin whispered, "No" and "I don't know" and "Impossible", close to madness, I realized that I could not wash properly, I could not make a fire, that the dampness and darkness had ruined my eyes, that the war was not coming to an end, and that I was surrounded by emptiness and delirium.

"Doctor, something must happen! I can't wait any longer!"

"You know that you are free. The unlocked door represents your free will. And what about your imagination? With it you can wander as far away as America, you can ride through New York in a deluxe automobile, or walk along the streets looking in the store windows. On

Broadway you can find food and drink and—what women! *Ooh la la!*"

"Stop! I am asking seriously: what should I do? Advise me; you have advised me so well so many times already! You yourself say that it is safer here for a while, that there is no longer a garrison here! Perhaps I could slip out at night."

"Don't do it! That is not a command, only advice. Do you think I am enjoying my own inaction?"

"My God, how can you compare yourself with me?"

"Don't get upset. I too could be doing more for—let's call it—righteous adventure. You thought I'd have a slip of the tongue then, didn't you? No, *mon vieux*, I'm sorry, but you'll never hear me say, for immortal France! You'll never hear, for holy vengeance, or not even, for the overthrow of the barbarians! I'd rather slap myself across the mouth. I say simply and truthfully, for righteous adventure."

"I don't understand you."

"Don't you know what righteous adventure is? You certainly don't believe that the people of Europe are regarding everything that goes on around them with the indifference of cattle being led to the slaughter? That omniscient gentleman of the London radio, the one we heard yesterday telling stories about occupied Europe, certainly had many Hollywoodish fantasies, an unpleasant beer voice and on the whole too little shame. But all that does not mean that an underground does not exist. There is one everywhere, and the one in France is probably the strongest and most extensive. Of course it's a little different than the gentleman at the microphone painted it. But now don't reproach me by saying that I talk like this out of my born antipathy to the English."

"I shall reproach you with nothing, but I beg you earnestly to tell me everything you know! Maybe I could do something…"

"Wait a minute. You're beginning to be romantic. That's a good sign, but unfortunately I am not in any underground. But I know a little about it in spite of that. But I am not a joiner. I'm a solitary adventurer. If I were a gangster I'd hold up cashiers without a helper, and if I were a prophet I'd perform miracles on my own hook, and I'd have no apprentice."

I snatched at his words.

"Doctor, couldn't you be more generous with facts and stingier with your commentary?"

"*Tiens, tiens*, why so much fervor, friend? And why are you talking so loudly? You jump from one extreme to another. All I know is that often at night people I do not know bring a wounded man to me and I take care of him. Then sometimes those wounded men come back to see me when they are well. I'll have to disappoint you again. It's no conspiratorial meeting. I don't ask them who shot them and where and they don't try to lure me into their underground rooms. But all that has nothing to do with you."

"Why not?"

"I am sorry, but a man forced to hide cannot be helpful, at least for the time being, to people who have immersed themselves in a wisdom greater than ours."

"What do you mean?"

"There are moments when our will bends to a higher will, our wisdom to a higher wisdom which is beyond us and which we cannot even measure. It happens when we unite with something—with a thought, with people, with some passion—I don't know exactly with what. But in such a moment we stop existing, that is, we stop thinking of ourselves. When a man becomes one with someone or something so thoroughly that his own ego dissolves, then he is afraid of absolutely nothing and plays with death as if it were a little child. That's about how my cured wounded ones are. I'm not much like them, and you are even less so."

"Then why do you help them if you don't want to join them?"

"Because I am a doctor, always and everywhere a doctor. One does not think about that, one doesn't analyze it: you see, there is an example of where the higher wisdom begins. You will ask me if I would treat everyone if I could always decide freely—M. Laval, for example. No, of course not; everyone is not a patient, no matter how he writhes with pain. Who is and who is not a patient I recognize by an intelligence which often is not my own. But all this is stupid chatter. To put it briefly, you simply are not cut out for a conspirator."

I muttered thoughtfully:

"What you said wasn't so stupid, doctor. Sometimes I have seen in myself what strength it gives a man if he is able to become one with something. Even if he becomes one only with illusions."

We were quiet a long time. All at once he asked in an unexpectedly tender voice, without a single trace of mockery:

"When you remember and think, what is it that you regret the most?"

"That I did not know how to observe!"

"Now it seems to you as if you passed by without paying any attention to real life, doesn't it?"

"Yes."

"Hm. And the thing that you and I call real life is something a man recognizes only when he has lost everything, when he is as poor as a church-mouse. But perhaps only then is it possible for us to attain much more than ever belonged to us. I can't help it [his whisper sounded a little ironical again], I believe in miracles, I believe in super-human deeds, my friend, laugh at me if you want, I even believe in myself and in you! We two together are going to do something splendid, just have patience! And don't think that I am a degenerate Frenchman. Listen, sometimes I am so self-confident or so impudent that I even consider myself a good patriot. A person finds love only after he has lost it, and his country, too, only when he has lost her. France was never so beloved as she is now. The millions with whom she went down have found her and worship her today for the first time. For example, I myself am head over heels in love with a France I never saw before. She is alone, hard, silent and wise. I know her from terribly long-ago memories. Then I know her from the eyes of those wounded men whom I treat in secret. Then sometimes I find her in our impoverished land after sunset, in the sobbing voices of the bells, in the taverns where there is nothing to eat or drink, and not long ago I found her in a sixteen-year-old black-haired girl. She was laughing out loud, but she could not make her face, her mouth or her eyes laugh. *Fi donc*, doesn't that sound sentimental? I am so in love that I should hate to say a word that would profane my love."

Days vanished, and weeks, months, many, many months. I suffered and rejoiced, I believed and did not believe, hoped and grew despondent. The Soviet Union was in the war and America was in the war. And my teeth started to fall out. And all my fingers and toes ached with cold. Again German firing squads spread over the land and again I was in terror for my unwashed skin. I suffered indescribably from hunger.

Once the Gestapo examined Dr. Aubin for four days; I couldn't eat or drink during that time. Then I lay in a fever for six weeks and was delirious for three of those weeks. I thought that I had changed into a spider crawling around on the walls.

7

I GOT WELL AGAIN, Hanichka, and I think that somehow I got used to my vegetating. It seemed as if my long illness had cured me definitely of my fear of the Germans. Besides, not one thing had happened—except for that four-day examination of Dr. Aubin—which would seem to threaten me directly. Moreover, I could no longer imagine that anyone could come to me besides my friend. I had grown accustomed to all my physical pain, but still I suffered whenever I was not wandering along the paths that led back to my past.

There on the ground above me, where my host lived and worked, poverty begged its way. People spoke of disease, of death, of torture, and most of all, of some kind of tickets without which there could be no food, no heat, no clothes. "It's strange," Aubin would say, "when you hear men, real men, speaking of nothing but food and cooking." I couldn't imagine it, although want pressed on me from every side. I could barely imagine anything that was going on in that life which was within reach of my hand, and where everything was turned topsy-turvy. I heard about the deportation of workers, about executions, attacks, betrayals and heroisms, but all the news was too full of action to penetrate my brain. Flight into dreaming no longer brought me the comfort it once did, either. What good could the truth do me—that truth which I discovered on my dreamy wanderings, when my hands were crippled and my feet lame? I tried to read Aubin's books, but not many of them interested me.

One day I was leafing through an English novel about marriage and unfaithfulness and the flight of two unlucky lovers from London to Czechoslovakia, all obviously described according to handbooks of geography and encyclopedias, rather than out of the author's own experience. The book bored me from the very first page. I was only glancing through it, not reading it at all, but suddenly I became absorbed in it. On one page the author quoted Dostoyevsky:

The fourth age is coming: it is knocking, it is pounding on the door, and if the door is not opened, it will be broken down. The fourth age wants none of the old ideals, rejects all that ever was. It will make no small compromises and no small concessions; you will not save the building with flimsy props. Something is going to happen which no one is expecting.

With growing excitement, I read this quotation innumerable times, and from that time to this day I have really read nothing else properly. I don't really know with which of my own thoughts and with which of Aubin's words Dostoyevsky's

prophecy was connected. I only know that it caused a pro-
found upheaval in myself. And everything that came after
was a consequence of this upheaval. It seemed to me that
I would be lost. For you, Hanichka, for the future, for any
kind of new life. For Fate had shut me away from the smithy
where the fourth age was being forged; I am forced into
emptiness and I know of no way out. It might be possible
to grow wiser in emptiness, but it is not possible to atone for
something in a void. From the bottomless well of loneliness
a mystic finally emerges whom people will not understand;
or a mad liar driven by a bad conscience, who will call his
long inactivity and wretchedness a struggle; or an eternal
wanderer, seeking through all the corners of the world for
the promised land, which has not been meant for him for
a long time.

One has to tear down the walls of emptiness and emerge
from the wreckage, stop being a spectator and become an
actor! Otherwise there is no excuse, there is no salvation,
for anyone who wants to change from a shadow of the old
world into a three-dimensional creation of a new world.
Not for anyone who dreams of meetings and returns. But
Fate barred me from taking part in the battles of millions, in
the suffering of millions, and in the death of millions. I am
alone, in every thought, in every feeling, in every pain. And
powerless. Why, why was I barred? If I stay in my hideout
until the end of the war, I shall never again commune with
any of the just, not one of them will recognize me, nor will

I recognize them. But if I leave my hiding-place now, I shall be killed. For nothing. By mistake.

Where are the people to whom I might attach myself? A ninety-year-old man in a wheel-chair is no more alone than I. He does not suffer, separated from everyone, and he does not die in separation. No, it is necessary to emerge, to wait, and leave this emptiness at the first propitious sign. Then let happen what will!

Well, I waited for the first propitious sign, stationed there at my pathetic observation post, the hole in the wall. I did not budge from that narrow chink, through which I could see a strip of earth, a broken pump and two linden trees. And I did not confide to Aubin that I was waiting for a sign, for a miracle which would let me open the unlocked door of my voluntary imprisonment and step out under the sky amongst people and their suffering. Oh, Hanichka, through what horrors led the path to the people for whom I thirsted, and with whom I wanted to sit at the common table of want!

One spring afternoon, standing on a chair and peering through the crack in the wall, I saw a child about four years old, a golden-haired little boy. He was playing with some kind of movable toy which I could not see. He was pulling it around in a circle. It had been a long time since I had been lucky enough to follow the movements of some human being for more than a few seconds at a time. Every little while the youngster shouted exultantly, waved his arms, stooped over the invisible toy, knelt down and then again stood up suddenly and jumped up and down in one place. It took me a long time to realize that the child really had no toy at all, that he had dreamed one up, that he was playing with a non-existent little cart, or a non-existent animal. My eyes filled with emotion. I must have smiled at my little double, and certainly I moved my hand along the damp wall in a slow, tender gesture, with which I longed to stroke the fair hair of the little chap.

All at once a short, stumpy fellow in a black uniform came up to the child. Without being frightened, but in a rush of feverish curiosity, I realized that I was looking at a German soldier for the first time in my life. That man leaned over the child and asked him something in mincing tones. The child shouted:

"I have a puppy, can't you see him? He's all black, like you! But he's going to grow up, he'll be bigger than I am; just see how he can run!"

The black knight took the child in his arms and lifted him high over his head. "Let me go!" cried the little boy, "let me go, I don't want to, I don't want to!" and he started to scream sobbingly. The German obediently set him back on the ground. The child started to run. He disappeared. The man took off his cap; he had reddish, curly hair. He scratched behind his ear with the back of his hand, and looked somewhere ahead of himself in hesitation. That man had many insignia and medals on his breast; he must have been an important personage. He shrugged his shoulders, turned his face toward me and came nearer to my look-out.

When he came quite close, my head began to swim and I fell to the floor as if I were drunk. The thud echoed. But I was back on my feet in a trice. Panting, sobbing and uttering incomprehensible, croaking words, I jumped back on the chair. The German must have heard my fall and had stopped. I was looking straight at him—but of course he couldn't see me.

Hanichka, do you know who it was I was looking at? It was Fischer from Broumov—you knew him, fat, awkward, squinting—he was the only German schoolfellow I had at high school. You must remember him: he kissed your hand whenever we met, and he was also at the last class reunion in N.; you asked him then why it was he had studied in a Czech school, and he answered with an ambiguous saying. Can you imagine how I felt?

"Fischer!" I shouted at the top of my voice, and he started. I jumped down, ran to the door, opened it wide, stumbled, fell, got up and ran on. In my head something was shouting, "You're free, you ran away, your hiding is ended, your imprisonment is over!" It took an eternity to find the door out. I kicked angrily into the gate when I couldn't open it right away.

Then we stood face to face. Under the sky, in a flood of sunlight, blinded by too much light, by the free air, and by a stream of tears.

"Fischer, Fischer," I sobbed, and held out both hands. His mouth fell open. He always did have a rather stupid expression and his eyes and mouth always seemed to be surprised at something, or wondering at it. I went right up to him. Mechanically he took my outstretched hands, but his amazed expression told me that he did not recognize me yet.

But then all at once his mouth snapped shut, his eyes blinked rapidly and then started from their sockets. He let go my hands, bent over, slapped his thighs, and with convulsive laughter shouted the nickname my schoolfellows had given me: "Pussyfoot! You *are* Pussyfoot, aren't you?"

We were both so overwhelmed and excited that we acted alike. I too slapped my thighs. And when I stretched my arms out to him, he stretched his out to me, automatically, like a marionette. We embraced and kissed each other.

"I have to go back again," I whispered in his ear. I wanted to go back only because I felt uncomfortable from too much light and fresh air. I could hardly stand on my feet. From the beginning Fischer had automatically submitted to my will and my gestures.

"Well, come on back then. Where is it? What's wrong with you? Take my arm! Pussyfoot—I'd be less surprised at death! And how is it that you have no teeth? And how did you get here? Boy, you have changed in those few years! Did they send you to work in the French factories? Or…"

He checked himself. Perhaps it occurred to him that everything was not in order with his old schoolfellow. He looked around. So did I. Not a soul was to be seen. We breathed a sigh of relief in unison. He looked at me affectionately and laughed knowingly and heartily.

"You're in some kind of a mess, aren't you? That's why you want to get out of sight! Just don't you worry; I'm not going to leave an old friend in the soup! Where are you taking me, man? Why into a cellar, what…?"

He had the good-natured, rather hoarse voice of a drinker. Its very tone was reassuring, saying that everything would be easy, that everything could be arranged. Not ceasing to be amazed at where I was leading him, he bombarded me with a volley of questions which I did not answer. I really felt ill; my heart ached, and my stomach, but most of all my head. I led him and he dragged me. We got to my hideout and sat down on the bed.

"Now, Pussyfoot, spill the beans!"

I sighed blissfully whenever he pronounced that long-forgotten nickname. He put his arm around my shoulders and looked at me sympathetically with his squinting eyes. I thought that my miracle had happened, and that I was saved.

But my happiness, heightened later to delirium, was the happiness of a kind of drugged dreaming. As if I were observing myself, as if part of my being were not present at this masquerade of thoughts and this holocaust of impressions. Probably it can only be explained by saying that the whole drama lasted scarcely an hour and a half.

Everything was unreal, the cellar, the dusk, and the fat black soldier with the face of a boy who was once my schoolmate. It wasn't Fischer; he was merely playing the role of Fischer. The way he talked, the way he threw his body into impossible poses as he walked, the way he twisted his legs into knots when he sat down. And it wasn't I either, who moved and talked. It was my shadow, involved in an impossible fantasy.

"Wait, you must have patience with me. I've just been through a grave illness. I'm weak, confused, and beside myself with joy. How should I begin? I don't want to cause you any unpleasantness; maybe you'll be sorry we met each other."

"Hush, man!"

He said those two words wheedlingly, and touched my chin with his sweaty fingers. That called forth the first unpleasant feeling. There was something slimy in his good-natured devotion, but his intention to help me at any price was sincere beyond all doubt.

"You people issued a warrant for my arrest in Prague."

Again his mouth dropped open stupidly for a moment.

"We? Who?" he asked, as if he were ready to punish then and there the presumptuous souls who dared to issue a warrant against me.

"Just a minute; I'll tell you everything, but first of all speak quietly until you know the whole story!"

"That's right. Well, tell on."

"It's this way: all through 1937 and part of '38 I worked on a sight for anti-aircraft guns. My chief informed the German military experts about the progress of my work without telling me anything about it. After Munich I burned all my blueprints and informed my chief that I had done so. He raved, but still he did not tell me the truth. A few days before the occupation of Prague I flew to Paris. That trip had absolutely no political background."

"There was a skirt in it, wasn't there, Pussyfoot?"

He took my chin in his sweaty fingers again and I moved over a little.

"Yes, a skirt," I confirmed indifferently and went on hastily:

"But my chief reported me; he thought I had run away from Prague to turn my plans over to the French. I'm not keeping anything from you, Fischer. Later on I really did offer my gun-sight to the French, but they didn't take it. They didn't believe in its results and it seemed too complicated to them. I couldn't go back because I knew that the Gestapo was interested in me. I knocked around Paris and lived as I could until France fell. When I ran away from Paris I got as far as this place and I've been hiding from you people ever since. Just now was the first time in all that time that I have left this hole. That's my story."

He took off his cap, spat, put his cap back on, pushed it far back on his head, and bellowed in the vernacular of the Prague underworld:

"Pussyfoot, you're an ox! Jesus Christ, you're an ox! Who's the so-and-so who's keeping you in prison here?"

"What's that? In prison? The man in whose home I am hiding is the finest man I have ever met. He is a doctor and…"

"A fine pig! We'll throw some light on him yet!"

"But for Heaven's sake, what are you talking about?"

Like a hot needle the thought flew through my mind that I had committed an irreparable stupidity. Fischer got up, walked around me in a circle twice, then stood over me and asked, in the indulgent tones one reserves for prattling to a child:

"Do you know, you old fool, that you can be home in a week? That you can get a salary such as you never dreamed of, and that… Well, you are a wise one!"

I got up too, but sat down again at once. The floor was sliding away from under me. I stammered: "Home? To Prague? You think—that—but—that…"

Now I was listening to him with only one ear. I was no longer afraid that I had done something stupid, I wasn't thinking of the conditions on which my return home would depend, I forgot the war, Aubin, myself. I saw only Prague, you, Hanichka, my return, the home of your parents, our garden, my library. But no sooner had the carousel of sweet images made a full turn than something in it began to creak. It slowed down and then it stopped for good. The image of return froze. It had not been called forth by a man but by a specter.

Fischer, walking around me, was telling who he was, what sort of role he played in the Nazi party, what kind of connections he had, and what a fool I was. Every once in a while he beat his forehead and squealed:

"An engineer! In our time! An inventor! An unpolitical person! And he, the idiot, hides!"

A strange creature, he expressed his love and tenderness in insults. All at once he stopped in his tracks; he had thought of something. With him every idea was expressed physically: if he had some kind of new thought, he stiffened or jumped up, threw his arms about or sat down as wildly as if his life were being threatened by continuing to stand. This time, in the literal sense of the word, he threw himself on the bed and sat down next to me like a toppling sack that might fall on the floor any minute.

"Tell me something about that gun-sight!"

Only later it occurred to me that he was testing me, that he wanted to find out if I had been telling the truth. But first I felt drunk with joy again. Because there still existed a being who was interested in who I was, what I was and what I knew. I willingly began:

"You must listen very closely; without pencil and paper I can only give you an outline of my idea. The first novelty about my gun-sight is its way of controlling anti-aircraft guns. One man is enough to handle it. He has a steering-wheel in his hands and a pedal at his feet—like an auto. With the steering-gear he follows the direction of the enemy plane and with the pedal he calculates its speed. But my gun-sight has something even newer, much more important. But how can I explain it if I can't draw? At least let me have a match box to help out. You don't have that either?"

Fischer's stupid smile, with which he followed the whole explanation, seriously interfered with the fervor of my words. I kept wanting to say to him roughly, "For goodness' sake, shut your mouth! Please be so kind—I can't talk when you sit there grinning at me!" But I didn't dare correct him like that. Besides, he interrupted me before long.

"You know, I don't understand enough of it to fit in your eye. But if our folks were interested in it, then it must be a marvelous thing. Look, stupid, I could get you out of a *real* mess, and this really isn't any mess at all. So what? It didn't occur to you, prodigy that you are, that you would calmly tell the truth at your hearing, except for a few details? Look, Pussyfoot, you went to France after a woman and you got tied up there. Why you did, we still have to figure out. You didn't offer your plans to the French, understand? The best proof of that is the fact that no one is using your gun-sight. Only don't be afraid, I'll be at all the hearings. Within a week you're in Prague, I tell you. You won't catch a thing—that doctor will catch it all for you. I'll take care of him myself!"

It seems to me, Hanichka, that the whole plan, if I can call that rush of dark feelings a plan, ripened within me in a few seconds. When Fischer spoke menacingly of my host for the second time, I sensed once and for all, in the person of the man who wanted to help me, a deadly enemy. It is really hard to speak of a plan, for until the very last minute I kept it a secret even from myself. It seems to me that I was in the skin of a cowardly suicide playing with firearms. The thought of suicide does not mount to the surface of his consciousness until the very end. It is hidden somewhere very deep, so deep that it does not even resemble a thought. But all at once it rushes to the surface and causes death before the suicide realizes what he has done.

Yes, somehow my soul split while I sat hunched over beside my friend from high school dressed in the black disguise of a stupid devil. It was as if there were three beings in the cellar: Fischer, talking with a man who longed for a return to life, light and earthly happiness, and then still a third being, horrified at this dealing with the devil, seeing all his snares and getting ready to get him back into hell no matter what happened. I held my head in my hands, looked at the ground and asked Fischer many questions. But I did not hear most of the answers. I asked him about Prague, about conditions in Germany, in France and at home, about his position and connections, about his private plans and about our friends from school. Only God knows where I got all those questions to whose answers I paid no attention. I thought only about the fact that we could come to no agreement, although he was speaking in all sincerity and although it was in his power to fulfill my most fervent wish.

"And why do you really want to destroy Dr. Aubin?" I suddenly asked him harshly.

"So his name is Aubin! I've already heard something about that bird—in Paris, as a matter of fact. Too bad that I'm in this nest for the first time; our meeting was a real miracle. I went out for a two-hour walk and by the purest chance I came straight to you. If I were in your place, I'd see the finger of God in it."

The third being, horrified at the devil, sharpened its ears.

"What did you ask me about, Pussyfoot? Oh, yes, why I want to destroy him? Well, because I want to help you. That's clear, isn't it?"

"What logic is there in it?"

"Don't get upset! Do you want to quarrel with me over some French pig? The fellow who hides you certainly can't be our friend, you'll admit that, won't you? And if he has the crust to hide you, then he must be resisting someone or something. And we're just going to cast some light on that something."

Our struggle was very brief. Everything that happened between us was over in a May-fly's life span. Even this was like a dream, how easily all my hopes blazed up and how swiftly the fire went out, with what unreality completely opposite feelings racked me: joy and sorrow, faith and hopelessness. My other self which only listened, watched and formed a kind of plan, recognized with vertiginous swiftness that the hideousness of the world I was hiding from was not in its outward appearance, but in its inner make-up. That the Fischers did not lack noses, that they have human faces and human gestures, but that they are afflicted with cancer of the mind and soul. That in the index of their words and feelings I should never find what I was seeking, because the alphabet of that index was entirely different from my own. And that their cancer cannot be cured. Either you succumb to the contagion of their plague, or… Yes, there is still another possibility! I drew nearer to it, while I opened my mouth to gain time.

"Fischer, even I am not your friend!"

"May a goose kick you, Pussyfoot! Don't talk so foolishly! I'm as interested in your feelings as in last year's snow! It's enough for me if you keep them to yourself. Don't I want to help you? It's too late now; I'm going to drag you out of here even if you don't want to come!"

"But, Fischer, I know what friendship means to you. Then how could you want me to bring misfortune to my true—perhaps my only—friend?"

"Don't you think you're insulting me? Some French bastard your only friend? I'm surprised at you! Just how do you imagine my help? Am I to make a man of you again, rehabilitate you, clear you in the eyes of the Gestapo, and at the same time let the scoundrel who caused all your trouble go scot-free? I see that a person has to talk to you in words of one syllable. I'll tell it to you straight! From now on it's none of your business what I do! And now do you want to fight some more?"

"No, let's not quarrel, it's foolish. But just tell me once more: are you absolutely inflexible about Dr. Aubin? That's your last word, Fischer, is it?"

"Of course! What are you laughing at?"

"Am I laughing? I didn't even know it. God, how strange everything is!"

"What's strange now?"

"Everything. Just everything. How I ran out to meet you, your good heart, your tender abuse, your questions, your logic, the thing you offer me and the thing you demand, what will become of me and of you... Fischer, you people are going to lose this war!"

"I hope you never have worse worries, Pussyfoot! Where are you going?"

"Come along with me, I want to show you something. Go on ahead of me."

"Where should I go?"

"Out of here, where else?"

"Good, I'm finding it hard to breathe in here already. Don't worry, old man, we'll agree in the end and come to a good understanding. Look, the whole world is open to you and you'll bless me yet. And your wife even more."

"You shouldn't have mentioned her, but otherwise you're right. The whole world is beyond these doors!"

We were standing in the front part of the cellar where

once coal had been kept, and where now there was nothing but garden tools. I bent over to lift a spade. I was icily calm. Only my heart was beating more slowly. Fischer was walking ahead of me. His foot was already on the first step. In that instant, the plan, which was not really a plan, was almost ruined. My whole past, my whole training threw this trifling obstacle in its way: it is shameful to surprise a man from the back! But I wanted to surprise myself first of all. And so I didn't give myself even a little time. With my last thought I made everything straight, compromisingly and rather comically, if I may use that word in such a horrible connection.

I raised the spade with both hands, aimed it straight at Fischer's head, and said coldly and mercilessly:

"Turn around!"

The order sounded threatening and Fischer must have understood at once. He raised his hands as if he wanted to catch hold of something and turned toward me; it was a face with open mouth and bulging eyes. I struck him in the forehead with the spade with all my strength, and then I struck him three times more before he collapsed. Then, like a machine, the spade fell on his head until his face was mutilated beyond all recognition. I threw away the spade, took the lifeless body by the legs and dragged it back into my burrow. I put Fischer under the bed and then I sat down on the bed. I clasped my hands.

"Our Father, which art in Heaven…"

I got up and opened the door wide. Then I came back.

I took off my coat and trousers, knelt by the bed and babbled:

"Now I lay me down to sleep, I pray the Lord my soul to keep…"

I took off my shirt and started to sing:

"Paris, je t'aime, je t'aime, je t'aime…"

I sobbed, swallowed my tears and choked.

"Je t'aime, je t'aime, je t'aime…"

Yes, I had gone mad.

8

M Y MADNESS lasted longer than all my life that had gone before. At the beginning, Hanichka, I told you that it was just then that Dr. Aubin, as if he were doing it on purpose, did not come to me for a long, long time. He was in Paris and one hindrance after another prevented his return.

Nearly the whole time I half-sat and half-lay on the bed like a soul-less bundle of meat and bones. The light which makes a thought a thought, had gone out. My head changed into an ant-hill; instead of a brain I had in my skull a repulsive mass of tiny, self-devouring little creatures. Of all feelings none was left in me but revulsion. Now I could imagine hell. Time, measured by tortures, was not of this world. Ages passed. And the emptiness of my prison showed its unearthly face. I remember that of my whole fate I grasped only this: under me lay a corpse and beside me a bucket of refuse which I must not carry out. And in this stinking place I was not alive and I was not dead.

At last, at last, I heard Aubin's whistle, and then I saw that in one place the darkness was blacker than it was anywhere else. I was not alone in the cellar.

"Hi, have you starved on me?"

I did not answer.

"What has happened? Here's some bread and cheese and… What the devil has happened?"

"I killed him. He's under the bed."

There was a long silence. Slowly my thoughts began to come back to me.

"Whom did you kill? Speak, man!"

I could tell by his voice that he was trembling with horror. And this unusual transformation of my friend electrified me.

"Come very close if you want to hear me. I have very little strength left. So. Here you are. Sit down… I went out of the cellar because I saw a German outside. He was an old schoolfellow of mine from the days we went to high school. I told him everything about myself. He sat here beside me. He wanted to help me, rehabilitate me, make it possible for me to go home, but in return he demanded you. I don't know why. You can't understand them. He called me stupid and an idiot and an ox. Those were his kind of pet names. He wanted you at any price. So I killed him. With the spade. The stairway must be full of blood, and here too. I didn't attack him from behind. I told him to turn around. That's all."

Aubin heaved a deep sigh. He was quiet for a while and in that time collected his wits. When he spoke his whisper was once more the whisper of the eternal mocker.

"Hm, at least you asked him to turn around! I find that very comforting. But what now? Well? Do you think that anyone saw you when you were standing outside?"

"No one, only he. His name was Fischer. I am so sorry that you…"

"Be quiet! Don't assume responsibility which is exclusively mine. I'm of age, or don't you think so? Rather try to figure out what we are going to do with this dead German; I can't bury him alone. You took my adventurous inclinations rather too literally. Next time remember: *il ne faut pas exagérer*. I was not prepared for a corpse under the bed, believe me. Do you have any clever ideas?"

"Maybe those people whom you treated secretly might…"

"I'm just thinking of them, but I don't even know their names, let alone their addresses. Wait, I do know one of them! I'd better be getting along again. I'll look for a gravedigger. And meantime you eat. I'll take out the bucket; there's a frightful stench in here. Was that German in civilian dress?"

"No, in a black uniform."

"My God!"

"He said that he was not from hereabouts, that he had come here by the merest chance, but that's all I know."

"There's nothing left but to hope that they will not look for him in houses and cellars."

"What did I get you into again, doctor! If you knew…"

"Sh, not a word! Or I'll begin to declare my love for you with insults too. Eat and wait. What's the matter? Are you laughing? That would please me."

"I'm laughing and crying. You are so… I was out of my mind all that time, but now again…"

"So long! I'm on my way. I should really be thanking you. A fellow doesn't get bored with you around, at least. Are you eating? That's good. I think I'll be back before long. That man doesn't live far from here."

After Aubin left I finished eating the bread and cheese, turned over on the bed, looked intently and gratefully up toward the dark, and burst into quiet tears. I was so moved by God's mercifulness. A trial for murder had just ended by my being freed.

I fell right asleep. I slept soundly and unusually long and I dreamed of people's faces and of people's voices. Finally I heard Aubin's whisper:

"He keeps right on sleeping."

"Then wake him," another muffled voice said impatiently.

All that must still be part of the dream. From where else could anyone but Aubin have come? I pinched my cheek. Was I really awake? I listened to a third voice, a little tremulous with age. It was full of fear lest people not understand what it was trying to say. The man to whom that voice belonged, constantly asked: "Do you understand? Do you see what I mean? Is it clear to you?"

"Doctor, do you ever tune in on America? I'd like to

know if we can expect anything from the New World. Do you know what I'm trying to say?"

"About a week ago I heard America. Short wave from Boston."

"Well, and what?" asked the man who had urged Aubin to awaken me a moment ago. He was some kind of chronically irritated grumbler.

"What I learned was very instructive and touching. The story of a carrier pigeon with a conscience. He was flying somewhere with an important message, but on the way he picked out a bad place to rest and there he had an accident, he soaked his wings in oil. He couldn't fly any farther after that, so—listen!—he walked to his destination. And he was decorated, and is exhibited in Washington, and the Americans use him as an example of discipline for all their soldiers."

"*Merde alors!*" the impatient one swore. "Wake that fellow up, so we can get to the point!"

Aubin leaned over me. "Hey, wake up!"

"I'm not asleep."

"You've slept twenty-four hours, though. I have some milk for you; here, drink it. And we have company. While you were sleeping sweetly and snoring rather loudly, I found some people who buried your friend. You certainly fixed him up nicely! He's lying far away from here in a forest. You will probably forgive us for not putting a cross on the grave, and for having had a very quiet, simple funeral. We also scrubbed the stairs and the floor. There were some ugly spots there. And you slept right on. The people who helped me came back to me tonight. They want to ask you about something. Sit down. But first drink the milk. Our guests brought it."

From the impenetrable darkness came a new voice now, friendly, remarkably mild, and immeasurably melancholy.

"You would like to get away from this place, sir. Perhaps we can help you. Dr. Aubin told us that you are an engineer and an inventor. We want to ask you about something."

"Wait, leave him alone for a while, let him drink his milk," protested Aubin.

In vain I strained my eyes into the darkness. I could see no one and nothing. The doctor held the glass to my lips and at one moment I thought he was stroking my hair. I felt indescribably good and light. Especially the words of the last person who spoke soothed my senses and warmed my blood. Obediently I swallowed the milk. The people in the dark were now speaking very quietly amongst themselves.

"At least take an apple from me, Augustin," said the old voice. "You'll dry up if you don't eat. When a person's on his feet all the time like you, he should have a full stomach, do you understand?"

"I don't want any," Augustin snapped. "I know your apples; they're rotten."

"Then light a cigarette. After sleepless nights a cigarette is more bracing than alcohol, you understand me, don't you?"

"Please don't smoke here," Aubin requested earnestly.

"I wouldn't smoke his cigarettes anyway. The devil knows what he fills them with. Well, has the patient drunk his fill?"

I addressed the invisible gathering in a rather pathetic voice:

"Ask me what you wish, gentlemen. I should also like to thank you…"

"*Sacré nom de Dieu!*" the wrathful and skeptical Augustin swore. "No thanks, there's no time for that. Do you understand ships?"

"Why?"

"*Crénom!* Don't ask, answer!"

The person in whose gentle words there had been so much friendship a little while ago, admonished Augustin:

"Please, let someone else question him… Just imagine, sir, that we had the possibility of getting false credentials for you and getting you aboard a certain ship as a stoker. That boat is going to sail after a time to pick up certain immensely vital material which it is necessary to destroy. The crew will be partly German, partly French. Would you know how to sink a boat?"

I rose like one in a dream. That voice, that voice! Does it belong to a priest? To a judge? It is sad, tender, and again passionate, alternately promising and threatening. And it is asking me for advice. I am being consulted! I can still advise someone! Is it possible? Can it be true?

I stammered: "Perhaps—if I had a bomb!"

"*Merdasse!*" hissed angry Augustin. "*Je vous jure sur la tête de ma concierge*, we are wasting time with this man! He wants a bomb! If we could put a bomb into the suitcase of the man whom we get on that ship, then we wouldn't be sending you, smarty! It's obvious that the Germans will search all the baggage and all the pockets of every new member of the crew!"

"Augustin, calm down," the old man reminded the hothead. "Look, sir. You are an engineer; perhaps you can figure out a way of sinking a ship like that without an explosion. Do you understand what we're after?"

"What kind of boat is it?"

"I wouldn't explain another thing to him," growled Augustin.

"Be quiet a moment, please! It's a freighter, not quite sixteen thousand ton."

"What kind of power?"

"Two Diesel engines."

There was a deathly silence between me and the people in the dark. They waited, scarcely breathing. In that instant it seemed to me that the walls of my hideout vanished, that I was out under a dark sky and that before me stood an invisible army, waiting for my words. On what I would say depended whether light would dawn or whether it would stay dark, whether the crowd would accept me as one of them or forsake me. The blood pounded in my temples with panic. I longed so much to say to them: Yes, I know how to do it! But that would have been a lie. I could think of nothing. I muttered:

"To sink a boat with your bare hands? But that… No, I don't know. I'm terribly sorry, but I truly don't know…"

"Too bad," that voice breathed sadly, that bewitching voice which had disturbed me from the first instant. My heart turned to stone.

Quietly, so quietly, the door of my prison opened and the invisible company went away without a word. Even Dr. Aubin left. And the door of the darkest prison closed again.

9

I T NEVER EVEN occurred to me that now I was in the gravest danger, that I might be discovered by the Germans at any moment, if ever they started to investigate in a wide circle, to discover where and how Fischer had vanished. After that nocturnal visit of the unknown people to my prison, I changed beyond recognition. I no longer wandered along the roads of the past, I didn't remember and I didn't dream. Walking from wall to wall of my cage like a desperate animal, I tried to solve, with the complete concentration of all my faculties, the question of questions: how to sink a big ship barehanded. I attacked the question like a rebus, like a mathematical problem from whose solution I promised myself nervous relaxation, a sense of victory, of peace and quiet. Not once did I think of everything that would be waiting for me from the instant I seized my head with taut, outstretched fingers and sighed happily, "I have it!" I divided my own personal participation completely from the problem that the people had brought me in the dark. It didn't interest me why a certain boat should be sunk; I wasn't interested in the cargo of the ship, its history, and I forgot that the voices in the dark had offered me false papers, and freedom and an adventurous voyage. I was possessed with the image of that living darkness where crowds were standing and waiting for my words. I heard myself saying to them: "And now that I have found an answer, take me into your midst! Relieve me of the burden of my body, unite with me. Take my will and replace it with yours! And share my suffering with me, as I shall share yours with you!"

Perhaps it was true, perhaps I only persuade myself now that it was: Dr. Aubin grew sadder during those days. As if I had disappointed him. He was taciturn and downcast.

"You have the devil's own luck," he said to me once without enthusiasm. "It seems that the Germans are looking for your old friend in an entirely different district. That fellow wasn't lying when he said he got here by the merest chance. The devil knows what drew him here! Are you saying something?"

"Where to get the force, where to get the force…?"

"What force? Are you still thinking about that boat? There's force enough on a boat, isn't there?"

"What did you…? Wait! Just one more second! Doctor, my head is bursting! Jesus Christ, hold me! Doctor, dear doctor, I almost have it, I'm dying with happiness, I want to dance or sing! Wait, don't move, don't disturb me! A hoist—of course—and cables or… Give me ten minutes!"

I was no longer walking up and down, but running madly around the walls, as if I were chasing someone. Aubin's quiet voice broke in:

"Please take your shoes off. I know that you can't sit down or lie down, but you're thumping like a rabbit. Now I'll be quiet; I'm bursting with excitement."

I really did take my shoes off and continued my mad race barefooted. Minutes passed.

"Hello, where are you?"

"Here, right beside you. What's up?"

"Doctor, I've got it! My heart's beating somewhere up in my neck. I have such a longing to shout hurray!"

"Damn it, your happiness is contagious; my knees are shaking too. You're not mistaken? That would be… Here, give me your hands, let's be sentimental just once; don't resist, I want to embrace you… No, I don't know how! Well, what of it? Tell me!"

"Go and get them, bring them here, while I get it all straight in my own mind. But you don't have to be afraid, I have it firmly by the hair. Go for those people, quick! Please!"

There was not the slightest doubt: I had solved the problem. And now I was only waiting for those envoys out of the darkness, to break the happy news to them. I found my lost self-confidence. Once more I was somebody and knew something. I could answer, advise, direct, I could…

What's that? Ah, what was that aching in my temples? What had happened again? Good God, don't I really have any right to rejoice longer than a few seconds?

Only then, a few minutes after Aubin's departure, did I realize that the problem which I had just solved would have a concrete performance, and that I was to be the hero of that performance. What a hero! But—dear people, stupid I, an incurable dunce, had just drawn the lot of death! All I had solved for myself was a means of committing suicide!

My enthusiasm vanished in hell. To die? For nothing? Now, when I had just begun to savor life again? No, not on your life, that's not why I hid myself, why I suffered like an animal in a trap, why I became a murderer! Oh, God in Heaven, is there no way out of my emptiness?

Again I ran around in circles like a madman chasing himself. All at once time began to pass too quickly, I no longer cared about the people whom I had so longed to see just a little while ago, I was wishing that Aubin would not find them, that there would be obstacles, that they would tell him it was too late, that they had already found another solution.

But all at once they were there. And a lot of them came this time, at least seven. Well, Thy will be done, Lord! The darkness billowed, the quiet watchfully huddled to the ground with light rustlings and whisperings.

"Good evening, sir!"

Oh, that voice again, borrowed from holiness. My heart grew quiet and my breath came more slowly. I got up on the bed, turned my face to the door and said chokingly:

"I think, my friends, that I can give you some advice. But first of all please answer a few of my questions. Is there access to the screw propeller on this boat?"

"Yes."

I recognized the voice of angry Augustin.

"And could I get…?"

I interrupted myself and corrected myself:

"Could the person whom you want to get on the boat somehow sneak into the propeller chamber?"

The invisible company started to whisper. They were consulting one another and coming to an agreement. I was answered by that old man who was so anxious to speak clearly.

"In the course of the voyage such an opportunity could certainly present itself. In this respect, one of the officers could also help you. He's our man, a good Frenchman, and he would be informed about you in good time. The crew, as you know, is not only German. You would learn the details later. You understand what I am trying to say?"

"Could you get hoists on board?"

"Why carry coals to Newcastle?" grumbled Augustin. "On every decent ship there are lots of hoists."

"And could the man who was to sink the boat have at hand a very long, strong steel cable, or an equally firm chain?"

I consistently avoided speaking of myself, but referred only to the person whom they were to get onto the boat. The people in the dark consulted together again for some time and then announced, interrupting one another as they did so, that there are many chains aboard a ship and that it would not be difficult to lay some down somewhere inconspicuously. There is nothing suspicious about chains or cables, after all.

I stopped talking. The silence was unbroken. I had been waiting for this instant. And so had they. Now I was theirs! I must forget everything else. Now for the last time let me realize what it is not to be alone! My own voice sounded firm and almost happy. I felt intoxicated with it.

"Pay attention, gentlemen! You have sometimes noticed how French railroad workers move cars about by means of a vertical cylinder, driven by a motor? An ordinary man throws three loops over the cylinder and the heaviest car is pulled along like a paper box. A similar force can be generated on the boat by a proper combination of pulleys. Your man will set and fasten the hoists on the main beams of the boat and will then connect these hoists with a very long and powerful cable or chain into one system. The cable from the hoists leads to the propeller shaft and will wind around it at least four or five times. The rotating propeller shaft will pull the chain and, with its own power increased by the hoists, will break the beams and the hull. According to my plan, we obtain a pull on the frame of the ship without straining too much on the bearing of the main shaft. Only one part of the assignment seems to me difficult although not impossible: to secure the pulley systems on the frame of the ship in a way that will transmit the enormous force without breaking the attachment. However, if you will bring your man to me, I will discuss with him all possibilities and give him instructions for any eventuality."

I stopped talking. The darkness around me started to rustle and buzz with excitement. Augustin shouted it down. He seemed a little uncertain, but still always angry.

"Listen, it sounds good, but it's nonsense!"

"Not a bit of it," I answered firmly.

"If you break the walls around yourself, water will not flood the boat, because it will only get into the chamber."

"You are mistaken. The hoists will be fastened also to the beams on the ceiling of the chamber, and that will necessarily be wrecked."

Someone started to applaud me, but Aubin quickly silenced him.

"How long would it take the ship to sink in such a situation?" the old man asked. "Approximately, I mean, one or two minutes this way or that don't matter; do you understand what I'm after?"

"I cannot say exactly, but I should think about a quarter of an hour."

"Would one man be enough for it or would he need a helper?"

"Gentlemen, you have told me so little about this boat and its arrangement that I can hardly anticipate all that."

"We ourselves don't know much, *compris*? We too are only half initiated into the actions which are directed…"

"Please, no details," grumbled Augustin. "This Czech is no fool, but just for that let's not fall into any premature enthusiasm. Could you do it alone? Yes or no?"

"Wait, wait, friend, let's come to me later. A dexterous man would not need a helper and two or three hours would be enough for his preparations. Of course, everything depends on whether he would be interrupted or not. The noise he might make will not betray him, because on a boat it is always noisy in the neighborhood of the screw propeller. And if there is some kind of agreement with one of the officers, it seems to me that it could be done easily. Only the unlucky man who does it will die. He won't have any outlet from the chamber when the water pours in."

I said the last sentence very quietly. I was loath to part with the atmosphere which I had evoked. I did not like to return from life to emptiness. Then I trembled under the soothing impact of that voice which always captivated me more than any of the others:

"And still you will undertake it, sir, won't you?"

I nervously pushed my hair back from my forehead and started to straighten my collar and necktie, as if I were standing before a mirror and as if a great deal depended on my appearance. The words tore themselves from my lips with an effort:

"Why do you want me to die at any price? Besides, there will not be only Germans on the boat; as a matter of fact there will be that man from your own ranks, as you yourselves say, and certainly a lot of good and innocent people besides. If the boat goes down in as short a while as I believe she will, many lives will be lost, and they will never know why, and of course I should be killed too. If I made a miscalculation and the boat is only harmed a little, or if I am discovered at what I am doing, the Germans will shoot me or hang me on the spot, the boat will return to harbor with her cargo and my death will be entirely in vain. I have found a solution, I have answered your question, but otherwise…"

After a short silence I added a sentence from my bygone life, a sentence which I had not pronounced in a long time:

"I don't agree with it at all."

Augustin raged like a madman. He hissed:

"He's giving me fits! Why did he call us here then and why has he been pulling us around by the nose with his jabber?"

"You have been shut up here for a long time, haven't you?" the enchantingly kind voice asked mildly.

"Yes, a very long time."

"You probably don't know what's going on around you."

"I think I know."

"Are you a believer?"

"Yes."

"Do you believe that everything that has happened to you so far was only chance? And that your reason is adequate to measure and weigh every occurrence and find a way out of it?"

The voice sounded like music which I had heard long ago. Somewhere in the mountains or on the water. I don't remember any more.

"Are you a priest, sir?" I asked shyly.

The people in the dark were astonished at my question. Aubin explained something to them to the effect that here in my hideout I very seldom heard any human voices from the outside.

"A priest? How did you get that idea? I am a woman! And you really believe you know what is going on around you, when you are so absorbed in yourself, your solitude and your own wretchedness that you do not even recognize a woman by her voice? Oh, no, your reason would scarcely be adequate for anything! Why did you kill a man who wanted to help you? Why don't you feel remorse? And do you know that Dr. Aubin, who is certainly fond of you, never once comes near you without a revolver? And that he would shoot you without hesitation if you were to become dangerously mad? Do you understand? But you wouldn't understand! I am speaking for the people who are here with you now, and these people speak for unknown millions there outside. Yield yourself to them! Try to do a big thing. If your plan does not succeed, well, it does not succeed. If you die, you die. But for a little while you will be a man, you will be one of us, you will be a fellow-creator of the days that are coming. Who are you now? Nobody. A mouse in a trap. And at the same time there is a strength in you which not everyone has. Of all the people we know, you are the only one who could accomplish this successfully. That strength does not belong to you alone; it has only been lent to you.

Do you have children? They too do not belong to you alone. You expounded your plan theoretically, but when it is put into action there will certainly be complications which we cannot foresee now. It may be necessary to go at the thing in an entirely different way—and who else but you would know what to do if the original suppositions prove wrong? Do not be afraid, we shall not press you to do it and shall take no revenge if you refuse. But we shall turn away from you and, with us, everything you love will turn away."

That voice, that voice! Now I knew! It belonged to my mother! It belonged to you, Hanichka, to my sisters, to my daughters! I devoured it with my ears, my mouth, and all the pores of my body. When it finished speaking, I was half-kneeling, half-lying, on the floor. The walls of my prison vanished. Once more it was the green night of my childhood. It was fragrant with rosin and pine needles. "Come!" whispered a voice out of the darkness. The voice of nurses, white brides and angels. "Come, my child, you'll see a little lamb and a halo and the baby Jesus. Come, the table is spread for us, come along, hurry, I'm with you, don't be afraid!"

I got up and went. Blindly and still surely. I found Her, the Mother of the fourth age. I found Her breath and Her hands. They were not work-worn, but they were unhealthily feverish. My palms were cold. I could feel the warmth from Her arms enter my blood. I whispered:

"I'll do it!"

They crowded around me. They laughed quietly. They touched me. And they caressed me. They had bread and wine, I had to eat and drink with them. I was theirs. This time forever.

10

DEAREST HANICHKA, I have been writing down all the episodes of my story for five weeks now. They told me that they would take me away from Aubin's not earlier than in three weeks and not later than two months. I asked them for paper, pen and ink, so that I could tell you my whole destiny. They promised me that they would take my notes to safety. Until a short time ago I wrote several hours each day. It wasn't easy; daylight is scarce in my cellar, and my eyes are bad.

I am so glad that it was granted me to put down on paper everything that seemed important. That means that one day you will know the truth. Now I am exhausted or lazy. I have not picked up my pen for several days now, and I find myself writing this tenth section of my notes somehow with difficulty. Besides, there is only a little to add. God grant that you understand everything. There is really only one thing I want to go back to: it concerns our common past.

You know, Hanichka, that night of our last summer in the country in Bohemia, when you slept and I was tormented by black thoughts, when I remembered your tears at the beginning of our marriage and the green letter, which…

Here suddenly—in the middle of a sentence—the notes of the Czech engineer are broken off. They are written in small, legible script almost without erasure or correction. After a long journey, the notes were brought to America by two refugees from occupied France who turned them in at the office of a Czechoslovak representative in New York. An envelope was attached to the manuscript, with the full name, personal information, and the last Prague address of the writer.

PUSHKIN PRESS

Pushkin Press was founded in 1997, and publishes novels, essays, memoirs, children's books—everything from timeless classics to the urgent and contemporary.

This book is part of the Pushkin Collection of paperbacks, designed to be as satisfying as possible to hold and to enjoy. It is typeset in Monotype Baskerville, based on the transitional English serif typeface designed in the mid-eighteenth century by John Baskerville. It was litho-printed on Munken Premium White Paper and notch-bound by the independently owned printer TJ International in Padstow, Cornwall. The cover, with French flaps, was printed on Colorplan Pristine White paper. The paper and cover board are both acid-free and Forest Stewardship Council (FSC) certified.

Pushkin Press publishes the best writing from around the world—great stories, beautifully produced, to be read and read again.